ECHOES OF NEWTOWN

Advance Praise for *Echoes of Newtown*

"Blake Fite has the 'Heart of the Father' He has written a wonderful book that will bring hope and healing to all that read it. A beautiful tale about a group of orphans and their adventures to overcome their pain. It brought tears to my eyes as I saw my children interwoven in the characters of Rascal and friends. Open your hearts and follow the stories of the Orphan Gang. You will laugh and cry but at the end, you will be glad you went on the adventure with this gang. Truly it is a must read for those who are helping children overcome loss."

John Moritz | Co-Founder, Hearts of the Father Outreach

"As an author of a kids book myself, I am pleasantly surprised at my colleague Blake Fite's ability to write a fiction novel for adolescents that is both entertaining for kids and helpful for them to process the loss of a parent. If you are a teacher, counselor, lay leader, or a single parent, this is a great book to help kids maneuver through all the challenging phases of dealing with loss."

Ken Kenerly | Author, *Milly's What Ifs:*
Eating Oatmeal Raisin Chocolate Chip Cookies

"My highest endorsement to Author Blake Fite and his work on behalf of fatherless youth across the world.

My wife, Andrea, and I have adopted two children from the Democratic Republic of Congo. Not only were they fatherless, but they also experienced severe malnutrition, homelessness, lack of basic medical needs and no opportunity for an education. They were living in some of the harshest conditions the world has to offer. When they are older and can more deeply understand their story and their transition to the United States, I am confident that Blake's book will be a valuable and effective tool to aid their self-discovery.

You don't have to adopt from a third world country to work with the fatherless. Here in the United States, many of our demographics are experiencing the epidemic of absent fathers. This will significantly impact the future of countless family trees in unfortunate ways. That being said,

Blake's heart is to reach and encourage those who have grown up without the influence of a father figure. His message needs to be heard and will have a lasting impact.

As a former college pastor, I worked closely with many young people who didn't have a father in the home. I have years of experience working with student athletes from the University of Oklahoma. Many grew up in the home with their mother or grandmother, while the father is nowhere to be found. For the young people I've worked with who classify as fatherless, I fully intend to encourage them to learn and grow from Blake's writing."

Adam Barnett | Associate Pastor, Redeemer Covenant Church,
Author, *Let's Be Honest: Are You Really Ready for College?*

"Having known Blake on both a professional and personal level, I attest to his unique qualifications that set him apart as a leader and, now, an author. Blake's dynamic gift of vision pairs powerfully with his ability to cull the ideal attainment squad, recognizing abilities in others that even they don't yet see. A far cry from "all talk," Blake forms teams that carry ideas to meaningful conclusions.

Most recently Blake exemplified the aforementioned characteristics in the assembly of a wide-eyed group of young people ranging in age from 9-12 whom he mentored through in-depth collaboration on the fiction work in your hands.

Echoes of Newtown chronicles the journey of a wily orphan gang through the real times and territories of the late 1800s. The students consulted on each chapter—each student empathizing with the experience of a particular orphan character.

This book is only a piece of Blake's greater vision—to bless orphans across the globe both emotionally, through narrative; and practically, through proceeds. Meanwhile, Blake's out-of-the-box collaboration process produced a freshly cultivated guild of burgeoning authors whose resumés now include a printed work.

That's how Blake does things—unconventionally, completely, and with an unmatched passion for the greater good."

Kate Fehlauer | Writer, Scribe Media

"As a former youth pastor and now a senior pastor I have seen the devastating effects of fatherlessness in today's families. The negative impact of this trend can only be reversed by the hearts of families being fully given over to the one true Father in Heaven. Blake's book truly helps kids to release their hurts due to the loss of a parent by providing a framework to guide them on their journey to recovery."

Jamie Austin | Senior Pastor, Woodlake Church

"My wife and I are raising our 5 children and as I stumble through parenting, I recognize the significance of a dad's love. As I work to love each of them well, my hope is that I can model and convey God's love. I read every word of *Echoes of Newtown*, and I was struck by how many lessons of God's love are woven throughout as the orphan characters navigate and search for the secrets to their past. This book is really a fun read and it serves as another tool to convey His great love."

Jeff Hoeman | President & CEO, Stonebridge Property Solutions, Inc.

"As a person who has poured over books and scripts for many decades this book is full of mystery, nuance, adventure, and tragedy. Bravo to Blake Fite and the kids who poured their hearts out into helping write their own personal adventure into the manuscript. What stands out is the theme of hope and redemption amidst great tragedy. This is a must read for any young person and their friends who are hungry to discover what the world has for them."

Jean Sears | Choir/Drama Teacher, Regent Preparatory School of Oklahoma, Founder, T.A.P.E.S Fine Arts Studio

"As the former Miss Teen America and a sixth-grade schoolteacher this book is perfect for young adults. I personally know how devastating it is when one of my kids have a parent that disappears out of their life. This book has a great storyline plus the discussion questions at the end help kids process loss."

Lacey Russ Randle | Former Miss Teen America

ECHOES OF NEWTOWN

A Novel

The Journey of an Orphan Gang
on the Shenandoah Valley Railroad 1882

BLAKE FITE

NEW YORK

LONDON • NASHVILLE • MELBOURNE • VANCOUVER

ECHOES OF NEWTOWN

A Novel

The Journey of an Orphan Gang on the Shenandoah Valley Railroad 1882

© 2021 Blake Fite

Published in New York, New York, by Morgan James Publishing. Morgan James is a trademark of Morgan James, LLC. www.MorganJamesPublishing.com

Publisher's Note: This novel is a work of fiction. Names, characters, places, and incidents are either products of the author's imagination or used fictitiously. All characters are fictional, and any similarity to people living or dead is purely coincidental.

All scriptures are taken from the KING JAMES VERSION (KJV): KING JAMES VERSION, public domain.

Feet, Joe Ellis Fite Used by permission. All rights reserved.

Wither Pilgrim Are You Going? Franny Crosby. Use by public domain. All rights reserved.

Safe in the Arms of Jesus, Franny Crosby. Use by public domain. All rights reserved.

Nobody Knows the Trouble I've Seen, African spiritual. Use by public domain. All rights reserved.

America the Beautiful, Katharine Lee Bates. Use by public domain. All rights reserved.

Louada's message inspired by *Chasing After the Spiritual*, Louis Ada Dorman, 1998.

ISBN 978-1-63195-007-0 paperback
ISBN 978-1-63195-008-7 eBook
Library of Congress Control Number: 2020901179

Cover Design by: Rachel Lopez,
www.r2cdesign.com

Edited by S. Kate Fehlauer
Interior designs by Audrey Dorman
Educational Consultant, R. Janzen

Student consultants on character-development:
Emma as Anne
Samuel as Billy
Ross as Rascal
Rachel as Lizzy
Olivia as Josey
Amelia as Rosie

Morgan James is a proud partner of Habitat for Humanity Peninsula and Greater Williamsburg. Partners in building since 2006. Get involved today! Visit www.MorganJamesBuilds.com

This book is dedicated to the fatherless wanderers of the world.
May God bless your journey home.

Table of Contents

A Note from the Author

Dear readers,

The idea of *Echoes of Newtown* and the Carriage Kids Book Series began back in 2007 in Virginia when our son was only two years old. The original title was *Adventures of Henry Washita*. Henry is our son's middle name and Washita is the county I grew up in Oklahoma until I went to college.

During the initial writing of the manuscript I was working for National Fatherhood Initiative. Between my wife, Laura, and I having our first child and me commuting back and forth between Washington D.C. and Chesapeake, Virginia, life was very busy. On our weekends before our son was born, we hiked in the Shenandoah Valley trails. It was on these hikes and learning about the history of the U.S. when we visited Williamsburg, which inspired the initial manuscript.

I wrote the outline, working title, and some of the initial story, then tucked it away thinking I would someday pick it up again. When our son was nearly three, my wife became pregnant with our daughter, so instead of writing, I was moving the family to Tulsa to be near my relatives. That's where I found and joined Change a Life Foundation, developing orphanages in Africa.

On one business trip with Change a Life, I visited the Christian Alliance for Orphans (CAFO) Conference in Nashville, Tenn., where I met founder of Hearts of the Father Outreach, John Moritz—a friend who would forever change my life. We instantly connected on our mutual interest in Ghana, Africa, where we both had helped develop orphanages. We decided I would check up on the little ones at the orphanages both John and I helped develop to see if I could find ways to maximize our time and resources.

When I got to Ghana a few months later, I was cheerfully greeted by the chairman of the board at the time by the name of David Kwadwo Ofosuhene. The development was close to the ocean in Southern Ghana. There were rocks everywhere on the ground and poverty all around, but the beauty of the ocean and the children imprinted my mind.

The sign on the main building read, "JoshKrisDan Home for Children." I thought to myself *Who came up with this name and why?* I later found out this orphanage was the main orphanage of Hearts of the Father Outreach. Land had been purchased in 1998 and completed in 2000.

John explained over the phone that the name comes from the combined names of himself, his wife, Libby, and their three children who had tragically perished in a car accident in 1982: Joshua, Kristen and Dan.

After the phone call, I wept for their loss. I knew I couldn't remove the pain (only God can do that), but I wanted to help further their ministry. A few years after this trip, I picked up that old book manuscript I started writing so many years ago. The time was right.

Echoes of Newtown follows seven orphans in the book and later on in the process of writing it three of them were named after the Moritz kids in honor of their lives, brief and precious.

Throughout the writing process, John and his wife Libby have been so helpful and gracious to answer all my questions about their kids. Please see the back of the book for two ways you can help support Hearts of the Father ministries.

Let me close with this. When it rains in Africa, it pours so hard it sounds like millions of people clapping. It dawned on me one day that every time it rains it reminds me of all the orphans who have gone on before us to heaven who are cheering us on to finish well. If you are reading this, you can help those who have lost a parent by simply gifting this book to them and inviting them on the journey of healing and restoration.

We can help—one at a time!

Blake Fite

Acknowledgements

Echoes of Newtown would not be a reality today if it were not for these:

To my wife of 19 years, Laura—thank you for being supportive when I would hole myself up in the office writing instead of helping the kids with homework and dinner. Also, thank you for your faithfulness in your counseling practice over our entire marriage. The families you serve are blessed to have you. I love you.

To the writer's group—Samuel, Rachel, Emma, Ross, Amelia, Olive and the Phantom Orphan used to represent orphans across the world— thank you for your faithfulness. The plight of the fatherless wanderers of the world inspires us to do this work.

Especially to my daughter, Rachel, and my son, Samuel—you two are such great humans. Thank you for being you and nothing more. Do not ever let anyone paint your canvas for you. And if anyone ever belittles your calling to *just a hobby* (even if it's me), then don't listen to them. Consider it white noise. *Disclaimer: Do tell your Mother your plans first.*

To my editor, Kate Fehlauer, who put up with my sporadic ideas— thanks for taking this book way past my own abilities and for sharing your daughter in the writer's group. She is amazing! Your insight, ability to keep up with my new ideas and your deep understanding of the plight of the orphan truly made this book what it is. Josiah, you are truly a good man for agreeing to support Kate while she literally spent hundreds of hours working on this project. Thank you both!

To our illustrator, Audrey Dorman—you are truly family and I am so proud of you for graduating from college with your degree in Art Education. Your artwork will make a way for you, but your art instruction to the next generation will change the world!

To David Stephens—I appreciate you and Tina introducing Laura and me to the "Abiding in Christ" teachings. I wove these teachings into the book and it came at such a pivotal time for me and for us as a couple.

To my publishing colleagues at Morgan James—thank you for educating me and inspiring me. A special thanks to Lara Helmling, my fiction novel coach, for giving me the blueprint for finishing this book. Your spirited virtual meetings encouraged me to move forward.

To my photographer, Trenton Sullivent—you truly are a bright young man; and your eye for the right angle, scene and pictures are inspirational. Not sure what you are going to be when you jump the nest, but the sky is the limit. Count me in!

To my podcast partner, Tim Turner—your communication skills truly impact the world. Since you've exceeded my academics, I guess that makes me your, "young chicken hawk."

To Ben Beresh at Valley Way Media—your ability to place the vision for the book in video form was so critical to launching this first book in the series. I look forward to doing more projects in the future.

To the parents of the kids in the writers group (especially the moms)—thank you very much. Your support of this book testifies to what moms sacrifice for the sake of the next generation.

To Don and Melinda Wooden—thank you for mentoring me for seven years as your Director of Partnerships at www.changealife.org. Working with you truly changed my perspective on the world. Don, thanks for going with me to Africa and for modeling how to change the world one child at a time.

And last but not least, to John and Libby Moritz at www.heartsofthefather.org—thank you for your friendship, financial support of this book and constant encouragement. Your triumph over the tragic passing of your children is a constant reminder that this life on earth is finite and people need to be treated with gentleness and respect.

Jesus in Me,

Blake

Prologue

A Letter from Sage to a Sojourner

Victory has a thousand fathers, but defeat is an orphan.

—John F. Kennedy

Hello, young Sojourners.

My name is Billy Washita. A few years ago, my wife of many years passed away, which got me to thinking. Pretty soon, I'll pass away, too. And, I know that, because before my wife died, I said, "My darling girl, when you leave I'm not going to hang around here more than seven years." Yeah, when she took off to be with her Creator, I knew the clock was ticking for me. So, it's about time I get this story off my chest.

Now, I do happen to believe in all that Creator stuff (and reading this, you'll see why), but maybe you don't. Wye, that's just fine. After

all, no one's story is yours but your own. And *you*, young grasshopper, will have to decide for yourself.

I was like you, once. When I was just about nine years old, I lost both of my parents. Perhaps, that's how I had so much love to give my precious wife. But, hard as I held her, she too departed from me. So, here I am—down here on this side of Heaven—moving forward.

I grafted her wedding ring onto mine as a sort of sign to symbolize that I'm on a trail of tears without my darling girl, but I'm holding her close to my heart.

You see, I didn't have any sisters growing up. Nope, it was just Dad and me up in the beginning—before everything changed.

My dad used to tell the kind of stories that painted pictures in your head—stories about Mom and Aunt Sunny taking care of people who'd been all bloodied by the Civil War. The women had a hard road back in that day, (and if you're a young woman reading this, you can think about what that would have felt like for you.) But this is a different kind of war story—one about orphan life and the gang of friends who helped me survive it.

Maybe you think you know what a superhero looks like, since they've filled comic books since the 1930s. But, young sojourners, my gang was the first group of superheroes. Don't let anyone tell you different. Their powers transcended human ability.

As for me, I'm no hero. I was a young boy with weaknesses, and now I'm an old man with even more of them, and I don't much care about what others think of me. (I guess you could call that a strength.) If I could go back and speak to that foolhardy young version of myself, I might steer him away from a few of his mistakes. But, you know what? They weren't all for nothing. The Creator gives us free will to choose our own path, and somehow, by His grace, that young man found his future when he found the secret to his past.

So, grasshopper. Here it is—my gift to you: every one of the private journal entries I wrote to my deceased parents. These writings will launch an adventure you'll never forget. I just ask one thing. You see, for much of my journey I was arrogant, flooded with pride and no shred of humility. So, please, read it with grace.

You know, the Creator chose the time and place for me, and here you'll learn a little about it, but there's just not enough paper here to tell you about my time in Europe and Africa. I can't recount here the treacherous Trail of Tears journey in Indian Territory that marked me for life. I can't even tell you the unbelievable stories of every other person in my gang, but, if Lord willing I have a few more years on this earth, I will. You can trust me on that.

Here's my parting word to you, little sojourner. Enjoy this life.

You're abundantly wealthy. Did you know that? It's not your skill or your money that makes you so. Life is odd that way. It's your inheritance. (That will all make more sense later.)

People will curse you along your journey, but you'd be wise not to receive those useless burdens. Odds are that the hurting people you meet are orphans—not without parents like I was, but orphans in their hearts. Maybe that sounds familiar to you, like someone you know or maybe someone you *are*. If so, keep journeying.

The good book says, "But with me it is a very small thing that I should be judged of you, or of man's judgment: yea, I judge not mine own self. For I know nothing by myself; yet am I not hereby justified: but he that judgeth me is the Lord." (I Corinthians 4:3-4)

There is a peaceful vine ahead of you, and just like I grafted my darling girl's ring to mine, the Creator longs to graft you into that vine that brings peace and provision.

Chapter One

The Birth of An Adventure

Ladd, Virginia

The sweet air of hot cornbread fills the air this morning and just about every morning for this old man. My children sure do take good care of me.

They must think I'm a pretty typical old fella. But, we all have our stories, don't we?

The aroma calls me to the back door where I find a freshly cut portion wrapped in an old cloth napkin—my favorite napkin, as a matter of fact, because when you look real' close, a scene of cherries faded by the years comes right into view. Life is full of little treats when you look hard enough.

With warm bread in hand, I head out on my morning walk in the garden. I reckon I give that vegetable garden a good 2,000 steps each morning—just me and the Lord. Someday, I'll walk in His garden, but for now, this routine keeps me going strong here on earth.

Out here among the fattened veggies and budding sprouts, the memories flow like a river. But do you know the difference between a river and a pond? Rivers empty out into another body of water, like a lake or stream. Well, I've never been one to go against nature, so I think it's about

1

time for my hidden tales to flow into the sea of the next generation. And, young grasshopper, that's you.

I sure do wish you could taste this cornbread—made even better with a few of these fresh tomatoes I just picked. For a long time, my mornings started with fear and ended with sorrow, and I thought those days might never change. But, then the railroad came along. I still remember that fancy new sign. It read, "SHENANDOAH VALLEY RAILROAD."

Something about that train chugging into town with loads of hope and pulling out of town full of possibility gave me the crazy-headed idea there might be something more out there—a way to see where I came from.

Finding Family

"I'm dying you know, Rascal?" Billy said to his friend as the hot summer breeze mingled with the tunes of the locusts.

"You ain't dying, Billy," Rascal retorted.

"I am. And, you are, too. It's a matter of fact. This is the *first* day of the rest of our lives," Billy answered. "So why should I spend it here in some old house putting up with all of this mess."

"Well, maybe we *are* dying, scientifically speaking," Rascal conceded, "but you don't have to go on and say it. Don't the preacher say your words have power?"

Billy's deep-blue eyes avoided eye contact as his thoughts rattled on. He did this to keep himself from shifting from determination into despair—that was one of many tricks Billy had learned over his twelve long years on earth. The truth was that his home didn't feel much like he thought a home should, and if he thought too hard about it, a tear might escape.

"Awwe, forget it," Billy concluded. "We got birthdays coming up, and celebration is in order. What do you say we see what the fish are doing at Mr. Picket's pond?"

Mr. Pickets pond wasn't just a fishing hole. In fact, pickings were slim as far as fish were concerned, but when the fish were scarce, the large green plot was perfect for a game of catch or a good long session of stargazing.

The boys always found just what they needed in the sky with its mix of constancy and whimsy.

"You know, Rascal? I ain't got no family but you," Billy said, eyes locked on the evening sky.

"*Sure* you do. You got your Uncle John," Rascal said.

"That old drunk," Billy scoffed. "He ain't family. He just owns the house." Billy thought back for a moment to when his Uncle John and Aunt Sunny shared a happy home—before John's drinking took over and Aunt Sunny moved north. He kicked the dirt as he continued, "He can't even keep his own family together."

"C'mon, Billy," Rascal said. "He loves you as much as your Pa did. He just doesn't know how to show it."

"Oh, is that what the director says before she sends your buddies out to their test families?" Billy asked, referring to the director at the orphanage where Rascal lived.

"It's a *dormitory!*" Rascal corrected. "And, maybe it *is* what she says, … but it's true as far as I can tell." He continued, "She says, 'We're all born with hearts that know how to love, but sometimes life—'"

"Well," Billy interrupted, "if beating on Aunt Sunny and me is love, I guess she's right."

"… breaks us clean in two," Rascal finished.

The two kept silent for a moment—each thinking about what the other one had just said as they fashioned the clouds into war scenes. Billy thought often about the war that took his Pa and wondered what it had done to break his uncle.

"The point is your family," Billy said with finality.

"Thanks, Billy," Rascal said. "You, too."

"Say, Rascal. There's not too much daylight left. You best be getting back before supper. Don't they give you extra chores if you're late?" Billy asked.

"Chores aren't so bad," Rascal answered in his typical rebuttal.

"Not so *bad?!*" Billy said. "Last week, you said you were up past three in the morning scrubbing the floors. Go on, get out of here. You linger any longer and your knees will be as brown as your eyes by morning."

It was always a trick getting Rascal to return to the orphanage. He wasn't happy there. But this particular night, a wild game of baseball in the yard made his return a little more manageable.

The Dormitory

"You're late, kid!" shouted a boy from the makeshift outfield.

"I was just—," Rascal began.

"Just get in position the sun is about to set. Over there. Your catcher," another boy directed, as he pointed Rascal to the white rock they called home plate.

With an impeding hunger, Rascal could hardly keep his *mind* on the game let alone his *eye*. *Whoosh!* A ball bounced right off his chest and rolled down the yard toward a construction site nearby.

"Get your head in the game, kid," a boy yelled. "And get that ball!"

"He ain't getting it. You know Rascal. He's chicken," another boy jeered.

"I ain't chicken." Rascal said, while he worked up the necessary courage.

With a quick mask of bravado, he descended the hill. In an instant, Rascal was overcome with deep loneliness. (There wasn't much he dreaded more than being alone.) His pace quickened. *The sooner this is over, the better.*

As he got closer, he could see the building was some sort of museum. On the wall, he identified the form of two young soldiers constructed from a jumble of tile pieces. Beside them was a high-ranking Confederate officer. He inched closer and closer until he could read the name at the bottom of the mosaic: *R. Hudson. Hmm ... never heard of him.*

Just to the right of the mosaic was a spear as long as he'd ever seen. Rascal removed his bifocals (a pair he'd found and adopted) and used them to catch the last beam of sunlight to illuminate the plaque below, which read:

> *Flint spear, 48" long, crafted by Choctaw tribe. Used for survival.*
> *In memory of Papa Joe and Mama Doris.*
> *May God continue to shine His light on your descendants.*

Just then, the spear took on a glow and shrunk to only a 10" long knife. Thinking it was the sunbeam caught in his glasses, Rascal grasped his bifocals in his fist. But the glow only grew. Without thinking, Rascal tucked the short knife in his suspenders and ran back to the orphanage. About halfway up the hill, his chest swelled with a feeling he didn't recognize. It was a courage *not* his own. *Wow, what is this thing?* he asked himself as he ran.

Billy's House

When the clouds at the old Picket pond faded into the darkness, Billy sat up and planned his next move, *I wonder if Uncle John has rummaged up his dinner. I could sneak in, find a few scraps and get to bed without making a fuss. If he's anywhere near as drunk as he was at the lumber yard a few days back, I want nothin' to do with him tonight.*

A few days earlier, Uncle John had thrown a few punches in the direction of the local lumber dealer who had overcharged John in error.

"It was an honest mistake, John. You know me," the salesman said. Then, *FWAP!* Uncle John's fist flew right past the man's ear, striking a pile of cow skins behind the counter.

I don't need that old man, Billy thought, as he gathered himself and headed to the Vogt homestead. From one hundred yards off, he saw his uncle on the front porch with his walking stick, drinking whiskey next to his rusty old knife at arm's reach. *Who knows what he'll say,* Billy thought.

A few yards closer, Billy remembered the way his uncle used to be before the war—warm, smart, mannerly—and the way the women of the town would gaze at Aunt Sunny in envy as her husband walked her home hand in hand. *I guess that man is dead somewhere inside the Uncle John I'm stuck with,* Billy thought as he stepped onto the property.

Uncle John looked up from his stupor. *So much for sneaking in,* Billy thought.

"You don't get it, do ya, kid?" Uncle John mumbled.

Surprised at the comment, Billy stopped on the porch. "Sir?"

"You're chosen, kid," Uncle John said.

"What?!" Billy said. "Chosen? *Who* chose me?" he continued. *"Uncle John!"* Billy said with urgency, trying to keep his uncle awake just a moment longer to explain. "You've never told me about Mother. What do you mean *chosen*?" Billy said with no response from Uncle John. "Awe, it's no use," Billy mumbled.

He watched his uncle's eyes close, marking the end of their exchange. As Uncle John faded from consciousness, his fist gently opened, revealing a shred of folded paper clearly aged by the years. Billy froze, took a second to strategize, then in one swift movement grabbed the note and ran straight up to his room without dinner. *Maybe it's from Ma,* Billy thought. It wasn't.

The note, written in the hand of his grandfather, read as follows:

The most rewarding part of man is feet without a doubt.
They carry the load of him along as he journeys and goes about.
One-foot steps out by faith to lead him to and fro.
The other keeps a vigil behind to guard him where he wants to go.
All his nerves go to his feet as a signal for health or pain.
They can feel the smallest grain of sand, temperature of the rain.
They're the humblest part of him. They obey his command.
Christ chose them for example to be washed instead of hands.
So, when I get to Christ himself; it's going to be so neat.
I don't want to be at His head. I want to be at his feet.

God stuff?! Billy rolled his eyes at the letter, ignoring his disappointment. That was another one of his tricks. If you look disappointment in the face, you usually stumble into sadness, and Billy had no use for sadness. *Grandpa was into God stuff, too, I guess.* He re-folded the paper and blew out the light by his bed.

In bed, Billy caught himself murmuring, "One-foot steps out by faith ... Awwe, shoot. That dang poem is stuck in my head!"

Billy set his eyes on the stars shining through his bedroom window and imagined his mother downstairs straightening the house while his father sharpened the knives. *Why does it have to be this way?*

All at once, a new thought entered his mind as if to answer his question. *It doesn't!*

Billy shot up in bed stirred by visions of the new railroad and whispered to himself, "That's *it!* I'm getting out of here. If Uncle John knows so much about me—wye, it's time I learn a little about my own self." Returning to his pillow, he said, "Tomorrow, is the first day of the rest of my life."

Resolved to plan his escape, Billy fell asleep.

Ask Yourself
1. How do you define family? What did Jesus say about family?
2. Can you relate to Rascal's fear of being alone? Please explain.
3. Why did Billy care about being chosen?
4. Why does Billy want to know more about his mother? Himself?

Outdoor Survival Tips: Share the Plan

Be sure to give your trip itinerary to someone who is not going with you on your adventure. Include estimated timelines and resources (like friends you'll visit along the way and stopping points). In case you experience an unexpected hardship on your journey, sharing the plan could mean the difference between life and death!

Follow Billy's Journey

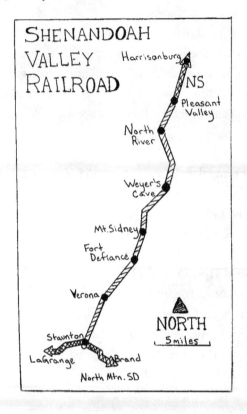

Chapter Two

Staunton, Virginia, or Bust

Preparation for the Journey

Dear Ma and Pa,

People wonder how I can miss my Ma having never known her. Honestly, I don't have an answer for them, but I sure know I miss you. And, Pa, I best apologize for my anger. Sometimes, I miss you so hard I just want to punch a picket that God took you away from me. Now, I know that fence picket didn't do no harm to me, but I guess sadness just comes out like that every so often.

You taught me to be kind, and I'm tryin'. Good 'ol Rascal keeps me honest when I get a hot head.

The way I remember it, you never threw a punch at no one 'less they were being unmannerly toward a woman or some such. Uncle John tells me you were human just like the rest of us, so I guess he remembers you as you were, while I've prettied up all the rough parts.

When I see you again, I want to hear about your friends and the trouble you got into. Oh! And how'd you meet my Ma?

With love,

Billy

9

The Map says "Go North!"

The next morning, Billy woke up with a fiery zest. *First, I better tell Rascal,* he thought. A loud racket downstairs reminded Billy that he needed to consider how to get around his Uncle John. *Guess he's stumblin' inside after another long night on the porch,* he thought.

He leapt off the bed and flipped around to face it. Lifting up his quilt, he reached into the darkness underneath the bed frame and pulled out an old army box that belonged to his Pa. *Let's see what we got here.* He rummaged a bit tempering his excitement with restraint so as not to damage any of his Pa's old things. *Just what I need—a map!*

Billy looked over the map to find his current location. *So, we're … here,* Billy thought as he found Ladd on the map. *And, Aunt Sunny is … HERE,* Billy thought, putting his right index finger on the black dot marked "Harrisonburg"—a few inches due north of Ladd on the map. Billy inched his index finger along the map, measuring about 40 miles between the two cities. *That ain't bad,* he thought.

"We're going north!" Billy exclaimed with satisfaction, slapping his hand down on the map. Realizing his outburst, he quieted himself to keep from exposing his plan to his Uncle John and re-folded the map along its well-worn creases.

"I gotta tell Rascal!" Billy muttered as he rummaged through the rest of the contents of his Pa's old army box. "A canteen! Perfect!" Billy exclaimed as he shuffled through other items: a few slices of old army soap, a partially used roll of medical tape, and a tin cup.

What am I going to do with a Bible? Billy thought, as he moved his Pa's worn Bible to the side to grab hold of what looked like fishing line. "Yes!" Billy whispered, "Line and tackle! Fish it *is!*" Billy continued as he imagined himself slapping a fresh young Bluegill onto a blazing fire.

"That'll do it for now," Billy said, as he closed up the box and slid it back under the bed. "I'd better finish this later, or I'll miss Rascal."

Without even so much as a creaking floorboard, Billy snuck out past his Uncle John and bolted toward the general store, where the boys had a habit of meeting over the summer months. Billy tried to suppress his hopes as he ran. *Rascal has it good here. Maybe he won't want any part of this.* But by the time the general store was in view, all of Billy's doubts gave way to excitement, and he almost shouted ahead of himself, "PACK A BAG, RASCAL! WE'RE GETTING OUT OF HERE!" Before he could, the clerk called out, "Whatcha up to, Billy?" Billy stopped and attempted to force his smile into one of those adult expression's grownups make when they talk about the clouds moving in.

"Oh, good morning, Sir. Good day for fishing, I reckon," Billy responded.

The interaction reminded Billy that he'd better keep his plan secret if he didn't want to get sent right back to his Uncle John's for a whoopin'. *Rascal and I best get somewhere private,* he thought.

"That'll be nine cents, son," the clerk said to Billy—now with a handful of worms wriggling through his fingers.

Just then, Rascal entered the general store, "Mornin', Sir."

"Morning, boy," the clerk responded. "You heading out for a fish, too?"

"Uhhmm—" Rascal began before Billy grabbed his arm and answered for him.

"Yeah, Rasc. I was just tellin' the gentleman here how we were stocking up for a good long fish out at Mr. Pickett's Pond." Billy shot Rascal a long obvious wink. Rascal was always good at picking up secret messages, but the important messages still needed a wink just in case. "I got the worms right here. Let's go!" Without hesitation, the boys ran down the front steps.

"Them boys are up to no good," the clerk said, shaking his head. Then, he hollered after them, "Ain'tcha gonna need a *pole?!*"

The Plan

"Okay, so what was *that?!*" Rascal asked out of breath at the edge of the pond. "You some kind of outlaw fisherman now? What's the emergency?"

"Rascal. We're going to Harrisonburg!"

"We're *what?!*" Rascal said.

"We're hopping a train and getting out of here. Remember, today is the first—"

"Yeah, yeah, the first day of the rest of our lives. I know, I know," Rascal finished.

"Right!" Billy said, pleased that Rascal had been listening. "So, whattya say we go to HARRISONBURG!"

"What's in Harrisonburg?"

"My Aunt Sunny," Billy said. "She has a piece of my story that just isn't here. I can't get anywhere else. Last I heard, she was in Harrisonburg"

"But what's the Shenandoah Valley got to do with me?" Rascal asked, still trying to keep up to Billy's big idea.

"Now, Rascal." Billy began. "I know you don't like it much at the orphana—err … the *dormitory*," Billy corrected himself, "but they do feed ya' right, so I understand you not wanting to get up and leave. But, see, well …" Billy struggled for words, "I need my best friend with me … to fight the dragons."

"Yeah, I'm a real *dragon warrior*," Rascal interrupted with a scoff and a chuckle.

"—but if you don't want to give up your hot meals for me, I understand" Billy finished.

"Listen, Billy. I ain't got no family here. I ain't got nothin' at all but a beating every few days on the ball field and some slop called dinner at the dormitory. Sounds like you're asking me to miss a meal or two, but by God, I'd miss more than that if you take off without me. I'm *going.* "

"*Really?*"

Something about the surprise in Billy's voice shot a bolt of nervousness straight through Rascal's unusually confident heart, so he responded, "You *know* what you're doin', right?"

"Course I do," Billy said with a false confidence that set them both at ease.

"Course you do," Rascal echoed. "Then, I'm goin'."

The boys sat down at the edge of the pond and looked out at the ducks zigzagging across the surface of the waters.

"Now, tell me." Rascal said. "What're we doin' with all these *worms?*"

Heading Out

After a few hours of throwing worms into the pond, Billy got back to business. "Today is Tuesday. We'll leave Saturday. You got supplies?"

"Supplies? I have a blanket," Rascal answered.

"Great. Bring it. But we're gonna need more than that," Billy said, as he scratched a list into the dirt in front of them.

Canteen

"We can use Uncle John's. That's just about the only thing from the war that he doesn't curse, that canteen."

Food

"Uncle John says an army marches on its stomach. I'll get rice, potatoes, onions and a jar of molasses. You get hardtack for making corncakes and some salt meat. The rest—like berries and fish—we'll find on the way."

Blanket

"Now, you say you got one of those, eh Rascal? Wye, I got one, too. If we can keep those dry, they'll be good for the summer."

Pocket knife

Rope

"I'd say about 20 feet of rope should do it."

Train tickets

"I suppose we'll get those when the time is right" Billy said. "… and medicine!" he added, finishing the list. "Adding this to all of my Pa's old supplies should give us everything we need."

"How do you suppose we're going to get *medicine?*" Rascal asked.

"What's that, Rascal?" Billy said with a sickly voice. "I can't hear you on account of my bum ear. I must have an infection in there pretty good—so much pain. *Ohhh, the pain!!*"

Rascal laughed, "We'll see if that works with the doc."

The boys spent the last few days rounding up the items on their list.

"So, what did you come up with, Rascal? Get us a few steaks for the road?" Billy said with a laugh.

"Well, it's not steak, but it's about the best I could pilfer without getting my backside in trouble. They don't take kindly to pilferers at the dormitory," Rascal answered.

"There must be *five pounds* of salt meat here, Rasc!" Billy shouted. "How'd you ever find this much."

"Well, the truth is I've been savin' food just about as long as I've been eatin' it. You know … just in case," Rascal said.

"In case' uh *what?*" Billy asked, still sifting through Rascal's sack of goods.

"I don't so much know exactly. You know, it's good to think ahead, and …" Rascal struggled for words. "So, it seemed if anyone should be thinking about my tomorrow, it should be me," Rascal said.

As Rascal continued, Billy remembered a handful of days when Rascal missed breakfast to keep away from the bullies in the dining hall, and a wave of compassion swelled. *He really is all alone at that place,* he thought. For a moment, he let go of Rascal's pack and looked right into Rascal's eyes with one of those glances that lets a person know you hear what they're really trying to say. Rascal took a breath and stopped struggling to explain himself. Then, Billy broke the silence. "You sure are scared of it all, aren't you?" Billy said with a laugh.

"Tell that to your stomach when it's nice and full on the road to wherever we're going," Rascal said.

Dr. Phillips

"We're all set! Everything is packed and ready for tomorrow." Billy said to Rascal as they met up in front of the general store.

"Not hardly," Rascal replied. "You said we still need medicine."

"Yeah, but that's easy," Billy said. "Once I get a look around that pharmacy, I'll tell you exactly what to say."

"*EASY?!*" Rascal said. "You call *fraud* easy? Maybe for *you* it is."

"It's not fraud. It's simple story tellin'—like in school. It's basically schoolwork, and you're a natural at schoolwork," Billy said.

The two crossed the street and walked to the sign that read: AUGUSTA COUNTY PHARMACY, DR. C. PHILLIPS AT YOUR SERVICE. As they entered, they collided with a tall man in a black coat, knocking his black bag to the ground.

"Oh, no worry at all," the doctor said as he reclaimed his bag from the ground. "Good day, lads" the doctor said on his way out the door.

Stunned, the boys stammered an incoherent response. Then, Rascal felt a sharp elbow in his side.

"YOWW*uuuu* know about … *coughs*, sir?" Rascal said urgently, trying to camouflage his outburst.

"Coughs," the doctor responded, "Well, there must be one hundred kinds of coughs." The doctor looked at the boys for a moment. "Do you mean to tell me you boys have a cough?" The boys looked at each other with murmurings of a terrible fever but couldn't string together a coordinated response.

"It seems we've caused quite a scene here diagnosing you two on the front stoop. Why don't you join me in my office?" the doctor said.

A sudden guilt crept into the boys' hearts, but they followed the doctor to his office and sat down.

"So, boys," the doctor said, "when did it begin?"

The boys sat frozen.

"Has your cough gone away and taken your voice with it?"

"Sorry, Sir. You're right. We ain't the sick ones. Our Ma just sent us to fetch some medicine for the winter," Billy said.

"That is sound thinking. And who is your mother?" the doctor inquired.

Proud of his quick thinking, Billy answered without missing a beat, "Mrs. Sunny Vogt!"

"Sunny Vogt? You must be quite tired traveling all the way down here from Harrisonburg." the doctor said.

"You know Sunny Vogt?" Billy asked.

"Son, Miss Sunny and I worked side by side in the infirmary during the war, but I didn't know her to be a mother?"

"Did I say '*Ma*'? She's my aunt, Sir." Billy corrected.

"And she needs medicine?" Dr. Phillips asked.

"Not exactly, Sir," said Billy.

Sensing a scheme, the doctor changed the subject. "You know, I remember the day your Aunt Sunny said you'd been born.

Billy's eyes examined Dr. Phillips. *Does he really know my Aunt Sunny, or is he playing games with us?*

"She must have been so happy." Billy said, trying to buy time until he could figure out just how much Dr. Phillips knew about his birth.

"Lad," the doctor replied, "If there is one thing harder than grieving in the face of joy, it's rejoicing in the face of grief." The comment struck Billy's heart like a two-edged sword—straight to the core—and brought a strange and curious peace. Seconds passed and the doctor said, "Now, boys, I'm afraid I've left a patient waiting much too long for my house call. If you'll please excuse me."

Dr. Phillips opened a black bag the size of a large cat and pulled from it a bottle marked "willow bark."

"Here, if that fever comes back, sip this 4 times a day, but if you find yourself in a mess of ivy or with a scratch that becomes red, apply this." The doctor pulled out a small glass bottle stopped up with a cork. "This is camphor," he said.

The doctor was out of the office and through the door before the boys had the composure to thank him. "I'm feeling much better, Doctor!" Billy shouted from the front step. "No need to mention this to Uncle John."

The doctor slowed and glanced back at the two boys standing tall at the threshold of the office. He looked pleased, even honored, to have equipped them for their journey. "God's blessings," he said with a nod that let them know their secret was safe with him. And, off he trod.

Ask Yourself

1. What items would you pack for an adventure? What are your top *three* things? Top *ten*?

2. What natural resources around you (i.e. streams, berry trees, fish, etc.) can you use to find or make food on your adventure?
3. What do you think Dr. Phillip meant about finding joy in the face of grief?
4. Have you ever felt two feelings at the same time (like joy and grief, or sadness and anger)?

Outdoor Survival Tips: Supplies

Carry enough food, clothing and gear to support your entire journey. Bring a handheld filter, so when you encounter a freshwater source, you can drink it without ingesting bacteria. At least one extra pair of socks is helpful. That way you have one to wear and one to wash. Dry, clean socks help you maintain healthy feet—a must-have for long journeys.

Follow Billy's Journey

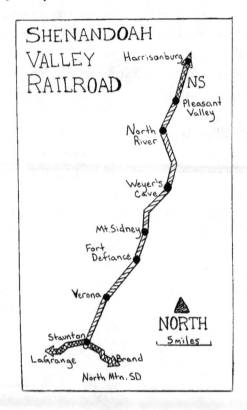

Chapter Three

Parts Unknown

Leaping Past the Hardwood

Dear Ma and Pa,

I surely know an orphan when I see one, but sometimes I forget I am one. I dream sometimes that I'm walking through the pouring rain when I come upon a house and walk up to the window. Inside I see a warm fire and above it hovers a black iron pot. Inside is a stew made from the most perfect lamb. How wonderful it must be to partake. On a slab of hot stone, a dough forms into crusty bread over the open flame.

I shift my gaze to the right of the fire and see a giant oak table. It must be fifteen feet long. It's dressed for royalty with intricately carved wooden bowls and metal goblets brimming with cherry wine. The center of the table overflows with fresh greens dressed with olive oil and twelve kinds of vegetables. Just then, an aroma of cinnamon, oats and sugar traps my attention, and my eyes follow it to a steaming peach cobbler.

A massive and loving presence sits at the head of the table. He is at once every kind of person, every tribe, every color, every language—all in one striking stature. He must be at least six foot, seven inches. Joy overflows from his delight in the scene and his desire to share it with those who would join him.

But, outside, I shiver. My empty stomach aches for food, but even more, my soul aches for the courage to join the table. I wonder if, soon, I might find it.

Your son,

Billy

The Last Watch of the Night

I've done this before. I'll do it again, Billy thought as he planned his final escape past Uncle John. *This is it!*

The hardwood floor posed the biggest problem for Billy. It always creaked right in front of Uncle John's room. Like most great plans, this one would come to Billy as he stared up at the boards above his bed. *How many nights have I dreamed right here from this bed.* Billy thought about the evenings his Uncle didn't take him fishing. He remembered the friends who were embarrassed to be seen with the drunk man's boy. More painful memories flooded as he lay in his bed for the last time. His brow furrowed. *You think you can trust a person … The only person you can trust is yourself.*

The nuns at Rascal's dormitory used to say the time between midnight and the last watch (right before sun-up) is when the saints should pray. The boys set this time to meet at the railroad entrance in Staunton, but before Billy could sneak out, he heard pebbles knocking up against the house.

Billy ran as gracefully and silently as he'd ever run. "Stop!" Billy whispered as loudly as he could without disrupting his Uncle. "You're crazy. I'm coming!" The time had come for Billy to face off against the creakiest stairwell in the whole Shenandoah Valley. As his feet neared Uncle John's quarters, a network of creaking sounds grew. They sang like a hungry street band.

This floor is louder than that ol' cannon ball lodged into St. Paul's Church in Norfolk, Billy thought.

"Zat you, boy?" Billy heard from Uncle John's bed.

"It's me, Uncle John. It's just me." Billy said in a manner not to further rouse his uncle.

Distracted, Billy stepped right smack on the worst board in the house. *SCREEACK!* Just then, three stray dogs barked.

"Get outta here, you dumb dogs," Rascal whispered desperately from outside the house.

Oh, for heaven's sake, Billy thought.

Uncle John sat straight up in bed and felt around for his gun. Gun in hand, he wobbled toward the sound of the dogs. Billy, choosing speed over stealth, ran out of the house and off the porch.

Two of the dogs fought each other viciously while the third, a regal looking animal, sat nobly by, unbothered.

BAM! … BAM! … BAM!

Three shots rang out from the porch and the boys ran into the darkness. The barking suddenly ceased. In his stupor, Uncle John missed the seated dog and instead fired a wild shot that sent a piece of shrapnel right through Rascal's earlobe.

Both boys heard the zing of the shrapnel as it passed by Rascal's head.

"He nearly shot us!" Billy said, still running.

"I think he *did*." Rascal answered. "My ear feels hot."

When they came to a small clearing, Billy examined Rascal.

"Well, he sure did get you. Some sped right through your ear, Ras! You've been *shot!*" Billy said, laughing uncontrollably.

"Well, that's a fine time to laugh at your friend," Rascal said, clutching his earlobe.

"Here," Billy said. He reached in his pocket for a metal ring he'd found behind the general store a few months back and slid it through the hole in Rascal's ear.

"What are you doing?" Rascal said, starting to pull away.

"It's a sign, Rascal!" Billy said. "You trekked through the dark woods. You fought off wild dogs. Heck! You've already been *shot*, and we haven't even left Ladd yet. Face it, Rascal. You ain't scared of *nothing* anymore. We *did* it! That's a cause for celebration, I say."

Rascal's body settled and he got quite as he thought about Billy's words. "You're right, Billy. I ain't scared of nothin—"

"Sshhh!!" Billy interrupted. "What's that sound? Someone's behind us. Did you *hear* that?"

"Stop it, Billy," Rascal said, thinking Billy had conned him into thinking Billy was proud of him.

"No, I'm serious!" Billy said with a hint of fear in his voice.

A glow in the distance caught their eyes, and a sinister feeling fell over them. Silently, they stared in its direction and detected a human-like shape whose orange glow emitted from the eyes. The figure was as tall as a tree even at one hundred yards off. As they watched, the figure split into two separate forms with the second one being much shorter—only about five feet tall.

"You still got that knife, Rascal?" Billy said, keeping his eyes locked on the orange-eyed creature.

"Yeah, I—*Wait! It's gone!*" Rascal said. "I must have lost it back with the dogs. Darn it all, it's *gone!*"

At once, another figure emerged, seemingly from nothing. Wings stretched out several yards from either side. In all of its grandeur, it leapt in front of the orange-eyed creature, rendering it motionless. With the speed of a hawk, the winged creature swept up the orange-eyed creature and its spawn and disappeared into the night.

The boys stood motionless and silent.

"Was that an *angel?*" Rascal said.

Still shocked but wanting to set Rascal at ease, Billy roused, "We'd better stick together."

The deep darkness of the sky on this night made each step more treacherous than the usually moonlit terrain.

"How are we going to find our way like this? There's no moor!" Billy grumbled, angry he'd brought his friend on a fool's mission.

"Look ahead. Another light!" Rascal shouted.

Oh, no. Billy thought.

"Let's GO!" Rascal said, grasping Billy's hand. The bright glow beckoned the boys. Before they knew it, they'd run three miles

toward the light without once looking down at their feet.

"We're nearly to the station," Billy said.

"How'd that happen?"

The boys paused a moment and looked down on Ladd behind them. A few dots of candlelight still glimmered from the little town—maybe one was old man Garrison making his way to the outhouse, maybe another was Rascal's old knife.

"This is as good a stopping point as any—only about two miles to Staunton" Billy said. "We got two fine trees here. Let's get some rest."

The boys sparked their flint to make a small fire. As they warmed their hands over the flame, Rascal said, shivering, "Maybe next time we run away, we do it at the beginning of *summer*."

"You got fire, ain't you." Billy said. "Then you're *welcome!*" he laughed.

Billy secured a sturdy branch between the two trees about three feet above the ground. "Grab some sticks about the size of your leg," Billy said.

The boys leaned sticks along the horizontal branch on both sides until they'd made an A-frame shelter that ran the length of the branch.

"There," Billy said. "Now that's a proper lean-to shelter—just like my Pa taught me."

The boys huddled under the lean-to shelter for their first night on the run. Maybe it was the wild dogs or orange-eyed creature or everything put together, but once Billy's head hit the pillow, his mind began to wonder out loud.

"He left me all alone when he took my Ma and Pa," Billy said as he drifted toward sleep, staring at the tiny slices of sky he could see through the stick shelter. "I guess He wanted me to fend for myself."

Rascal kept quite as he usually did when Billy got personal until something stirred up within him that had him speaking before he could stop himself. "Wye, now you wait a minute, Billy! You got a raw hand in this life, that's true. But if we're just talking about hardship, there's enough to go around. Now, didn't your Pa lose a wife when your Ma passed? You said it yourself how he pushed forward to raise you up until the war took 'em. Now how is a Pa able to do that. Maybe *that's* God givin' instead of takin'."

Billy listened without interruption, still staring upward.

"Billy, you *ain't* dead, and you ain't *alone*, so let's get that straight. If God wanted you to fend for yourself, you'd be dog food right about now, remember?" Rascal said.

Rascal surprised himself with his outburst but also found it satisfying. "Seems the more evil we see, the better God looks to me," Rascal mumbled. He wasn't sure if Billy would pat him on the shoulder or punch him in the mouth, but Billy did neither. They both pulled their blankets around themselves tightly and without another word fell asleep to the distant call of coyotes.

The First Morning

The boys woke with the sounds of nature. Birds chirped. Squirrels chased and jumped and dug. Somehow in nature, every character knew just what to do. Groggily, Billy slowly opened his eyes, then he jumped so abruptly that his head knocked several sticks out of the shelter.

"DOG!" Billy yelled, paddling his feet back and forth to get the animal off of his leg.

The dog calmly removed himself to the corner of the shelter where he sat up tall and looked at Billy. By this time, Rascal had opened his eyes and tried to catch up on the action.

"I guess he followed us," Rascal finally said. "That's the dog from your Uncle John's." Rascal reached up to the ring in his ear and remembered the events of the night before. Then, he reached a hand over for the dog to sniff. "See, this dog's no trouble."

Billy relaxed and pet the dog. "So, you just come in here like the king, huh?"

"Yeah," laughed Rascal. "He's Rex the King."

"Well, keep up, Rex the King. We're heading to Staunton!" Billy said.

The boys rolled up their blankets and ducked to make their way out of the shelter. As Rascal slid his knee forward to crawl out, he felt a long flat rock beneath where his head had been all night.

"Look at this." Rascal said, running his fingers under the edge of the rock to release it from the ground. "It's a knife—a *real* knife. A *giant* knife!" Rascal pulled from the dirt an unflawed section of flint about 10 inches long. It was the same knife he found at the museum. *How did that knife get here,* thought Rascal? It was perfectly straight with precise tolerance and balance—something he'd learned about at the dormitory.

"What do you know about *knives*?" Billy said, sarcastically.

"I know I've never seen one more perfect than *this*," Rascal said.

"It's dull as a rock," Billy retorted.

"The *balance!* The *tolerance!* It's unnatural. It's ... *super*natural!" Rascal continued. He took hold of one of the larger limbs from the lean-to and lifted the knife to it. "Let's see what you can do," Rascal whispered quietly to himself. As Billy packed up and headed away from the shelter, Rascal snuck a hidden moment to test the knife in action. As willingly as a cooked carrot, the thick limb gave way to the blade, and a strong sense of confidence fell over Rascal.

"Holy *smokes!*" Rascal said under his breath, wide-eyed with excitement. Rascal had a habit of secretly tucking away items that seemed worthless to others, and while this item may have seemed nothing more than a dull hunk of rock to Billy, Rascal saw treasure. He wrapped the knife in a small strip of leather he'd salvaged from an old shoe. *I knew this would come in handy!* Then, he rushed to catch up.

This Is Staunton

"Here!" Billy called as he tossed Rascal an apple. "People everywhere, Rasc. Eat up. We must be getting close." It wasn't 200 steps more before the boys were surrounded by all manner of travelers—merchants and artisans, farmers and families—everyone walking with direction. "So, this is Staunton." Billy stated with a hint of wonder.

"NEXT STOP, VERONA!" a voice shouted from behind a small window. A stately man with a hat marked "S" for Staunton spoke directly at the boys as they inched toward the window. "Yes, boys. Step right up to punch your ticket to the future."

"It's like he *knows,*" Rascal whispered to Billy.

"Two tickets to Verona, Sir." Billy said, as he placed his tickets on the sill for validation.

"You're just in time," gentlemen. "Now, we don't want your parents jumping from the train to track you down. You best hurry aboard."

"Yessir," Billy answered. The boys lugged their haversacks up the iron stairs to their seats.

"Rex!" Rascal exclaimed, seeing the dog looking at the boys from the train platform with unmistakable disappointment in his eyes.

"Let him go," Billy said. "People leave. It's part of life."

"But we don't have to leave *him!*" Rascal answered.

"What has happened to you, Rascal? Ever since you found that knife, you—" Billy stopped abruptly.

"STOP THIS TRAIN!" Rascal shouted. He ran to the front of the train and reached up for the conductor's horn.

"Young man. That's a ticket to state penitentiary," an ominous looking conductor said.

As train workers began to gather around, the boys grabbed their bags and hopped off the train, running toward the rear most car, past about 25 passenger cars, with Rex running close behind. As they ran, the train woke from its slumber and began to roll forward. The last car was flat with no walls or roof. It was loaded with heavy goods nestled tightly together. The boys threw their bags aboard.

"This is crazy," Rascal yelled above the dull roar of the train. "I can't get Rex on board while the train is moving. I'm sorry, Billy. I just cost us our seats."

"You get up there," Billy directed. Rascal pulled himself aboard. "C'MON BOY!" Billy called from the bottom rung of the railcar step, clinging tightly to the ladder with his left arm as his body reached toward the dog. Rex leapt into Billy's right arm. "Good, boy, Rex! Good boy!"

"Well, you might be crazy, Rascal, but you did it. You saved Rex the King *and* won us a ticket to good eating," Billy said, concealing his fatherly pride in Rascal's wild antics. "Looks like we're bunking with fresh war rations—boiled beef and hardtack. Dig in!"

Ask Yourself

1. Billy has a dream to make it to Harrisonburg. What is your dream?
2. Rascal has had to face his fears on this journey. What is your greatest fear?
3. If your parent or guardian could take you on a trip anywhere, where would you want to go?
4. Billy seemed okay with leaving Rex at the station, but when it looked like Rex wouldn't make it, Billy didn't give up. Why do you think Billy changed his attitude?

Outdoor Survival Tips: Make Shelter

When you construct a shelter, take advantage of natural overhangs for warmth and protection. If no natural overhangs are available, construct a lean-to with limbs leaned against each other to form an "A." The lean-to shelter is simple, strong and quick to assemble. Add leaves for insulation. Pine needles make excellent bedding!

Follow Billy's Journey

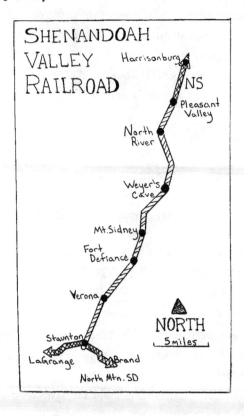

Chapter Four

Verona, Virginia

Anne of Berryhill

Dear Ma and Pa,

We're south of the railroad tracks around Skymont, Virginia, near a town called Berryhill. I can't believe we're already 9 miles past Verona station. The journey has been long, and we're pretty tired, but there's something different about this trip that has given us both a new courage. Is it just our own bravery?

There's a girl here who seems different from the curls-and-lace girls back in Ladd. From a distance, I saw her press her fist to the chin of a boy who tried to swipe bread from an old woman's sack. That's the kind of toughness you usually only see in the orphanage. She wore overalls just like mine and travelled with a dog she called Virginia (Real original).

I'm thinking this girl—Anne, they call her—might be a problem for us if'n we need to sneak a roll or two, ourselves. So, I'd better get to know this Anne.

Love always,

Billy

29

Time for Work

"Mind your pace, dear. The day's sunlight is not at your leisure," Anne heard her aunt call from their shared home as she headed to the general store for work. *The sun, itself, isn't even up yet!* Anne thought as she called back, "Yes, Lady Kathryn!" and increased her pace toward town.

By 5 AM (about 50 minutes before the August sunrise in Berryhill), Anne was already hard at work, stocking shelves and marking inventory. A few remaining summer wildflowers found their way into her pocket on the journey to work, and every few hours, she'd pause her tasks to smell them.

Sometimes, when Anne finished her work with time to spare, she journaled. On this day, she finished a book she'd borrowed from the school's collection before the summer break. So, she ran over to the schoolhouse to place the book inside the classroom. She rushed back to the store, so Lady Kathryn wouldn't find her missing. On the way, she checked a nearby peach tree for any remaining fruit. "All gone," she said to herself. She re-entered the general store where she worked until sunset.

June days brought nearly 16 hours of sunlight, but, by August, another hour of darkness had crept in—for which Anne was grateful, because her workday followed the sun's.

Most days were just about like this one. Before sunrise, farmers entered the store to purchase animal feed and fencing supplies. Anne greeted them all with a smile.

"Good morning, Mr. Rider!" Anne said, as she flipped the wooden panel sign to display the phrase "OPEN for BUSINESS" to passersby. Later that day, a young brown-skinned girl about Anne's age entered the store.

"What's your name?" Anne asked the girl.

"You can call me Josey," the girl said.

Anne smiled. "Nice to meet you, Josey. Is that a necklace sparkling under your collar?"

Josey grabbed at her throat abruptly to find the chain with her fingers and tucked the necklace back below the collar of her dress. "Oh, no. It's an old—It's nothing. And, do you carry *lard* for sale?" Josey asked, changing the subject.

"Not here, no," Anne answered. "Just down the street, the baker trades lard in large quantities. Forgive me for not fetching some for you, but I need to check on something. Lady Kathryn, my aunt, she owns this store, and it's unusual for her not to have arrived by this time of day. I'm concerned she may not be feeling well."

"Of course," Josey replied.

Alone Again

Just then, a boy called from in front of the store. It was the town doctor's son. "Lady Kathryn is in a bad way, Anne. My father is with her now. I'll watch the store. You'd better get home," he said.

Anne ran home to find the doctor sitting by Lady Kathryn's bedside. "She's left us, Anne," the doctor said. "She passed peacefully."

Anne crumbled to the floor and cradled her head in her knees. Her relationship with Lady Kathryn had been tepid at best, but with Lady Kathryn gone, Anne's dreadful imaginings took over. *What happens to me now?*

Lady Kathryn

Lady Kathryn, a refined woman, took Anne into her home at the young age of eight when the war, as war does, snuffed out the lives of her parents. She quickly replaced Anne's interest in flowers with gardening chores. "Only food is worth growing," Lady Kathryn would say. And, she had a switch ready to slap Anne's fingers anytime unrefined laughter would slip out. "We are not animals that we would screech," Kathryn would say.

For six months after the passing of Anne's father, Anne enjoyed time living with her grandmother—a loving, gracious woman, feeble in age. Knowing all of the extended members of Anne's family lived far away in Germany, Anne's grandmother desperately wanted to ensure that Anne go to family after her passing—not to an orphanage.

As a favor to Anne's grandmother (Lady Kathryn's mother and the only person whom she loved), Lady Kathryn reluctantly promised to bring Anne into her home.

Any bit of natural warmth that Lady Kathryn may have had had frozen over long before she met Anne. Some townsfolk said the death of Lady Kathryn's fiancé calloused her to the world at the early age of 17, and Anne had compassion for that. When waves of grief swept over Anne, Lady Kathryn always said, "There is no place for grief in a world of the living." How healing a hug would have been for both of them, Anne often thought, but Anne hugged her pillow instead.

Anne remembered times with her Dad before the war—the way he scooped her up into the air after a long day's work. He always smelled like grass and wild onion after his walk through the fields. Remembering the way he loved her, it was no surprise when she learned that he'd been shot trying to save two young girls caught between warring soldiers. She always pretended he'd died saving her. Somehow, that helped.

Life with Lady Kathryn was utilitarian. People were useful more than they were meaningful. Because Anne could run the store, Lady Kathryn was able to travel. Once, after the post-mortem publishing of a work by the late Ludwig van Beethoven (40 years deceased at the time), Lady Kathryn traveled to Bonn, Germany, to purchase a copy of the newly released work. She returned with a stack of papers so highly treasured, she would only bring them out on Sunday to practice.

Though her fingers stiffened with age, Lady Kathryn was an accomplished pianist, and this attribute, she passed on to Anne. Somehow, when Lady Kathryn taught piano, her rough edges disappeared. Her cynicism gave way to contentment—even joy. One Sunday, Lady Kathryn opened the wooden box next to her piano. "Anne, come here, child," she said. "You don't know what this is, and you surely cannot appreciate it, but, here. It's yours."

Anne stood, stunned.

"Well, what are you waiting for. Do you not play?!" Lady Kathryn said.

Anne, who had been at the tutelage of Lady Kathryn for nearly six years by this time began to play. Music wielded a transformational power that mere words could not. As soon as the notes rang out, Lady Kathryn softened. Anne's heart floated with approval. She reached the end of the song and reorganized the sheets of paper, seeing the title page for the first time. "*FUR ELISE, Ludwig van Beethoven, 1810. Published 1867.*" This was one recent pastime Anne did not mind remembering.

With the doctor looking on, Anne cried as she considered that she might be placed in an orphanage. Her tears expressed the pain of the loss of her parents and her grandmother—not her aunt—but the doctor didn't know that.

"Anne, I'm so sorry," the doctor said in consolation. "I'll alert the pastor to come by this evening to help you collect your things."

Anne knew pastor Jim and his wife Lisa from Sunday services, which Lady Kathryn mandated out of pure social obligation. They had several children whom, Anne observed, reserved their orneriness for outside of the church walls. The parsonage (that is, the home the church provides for its pastor) was quaint with just enough space for the people it housed. The pastor's wife, Lisa, a self-taught seamstress, wrought simple clothing repairs for people when she wasn't cooking or working in the small garden behind the home.

The home, though cozy, was not suitable for Anne to stay indefinitely. She worried each morning that she'd wake up to see the orphanage master ready to take her to the orphanage. She worried she'd need to leave in a hurry and wouldn't be able to collect all of her items she had brought with her to the parsonage from Lady Kathryn's. To ease her anxiety and make sure she wouldn't forget anything important if she had to leave in a hurry, she listed her things:

1. Coffee can of family pictures
2. Clothes
3. Thimble collection
4. My letter

The letter had traveled with Anne since the passing of her father when Anne's grandmother secretly ensured that the letter make its way safely into Anne's care. In fact, Lady Kathryn had no idea it existed.

For almost six years, Anne abided by the letter's red-letter instruction: Do not open until the age of eighteen. But now, with Lady Kathryn gone, Anne wondered, *who is left to mind? Almost seven years I've carried this inheritance letter—can't I know my own inheritance?* Anne thought.

Anne slid a thin piece of bark along the edge of the envelope to create an opening. Carefully, she removed the contents—a single sheet of paper folded to a quarter of its original size. She unfolded the brownish paper and read:

> *To the kin of MR. FRANK HUDSON, the following bequest is yours legally upon the death of your preceding relatives or at the time of your eighteenth birthday, whichever occurs first:*
> *One collection of silver*
> *One collection of thimbles*
> *One quilt*
> *U.S. currency in the amount of $31,624, redeemable at Farmers & Merchants Bank*
> *One book of Greek mythology*
> *Five percent shares of the Shenandoah Valley Railroad*
> *The aforementioned items remain in the care of the trustee until the point of recipient's eighteenth birthday. Until such time, the trustee shall remain anonymous.*

Thimble collection? My thimble collection? Anne thought. *Wye, I already have that.*

Anne didn't recognize most of the items, but the thimbles she knew well. She'd received them anonymously as a package a few years prior. She bent down to her bedside and felt around under her mattress for the thin, long case. The latches had always been tricky, but after a few tries, the case popped open with a *SNAP!* A small white paper puffed out of the case and drifted to the ground.

"Oh, no! A label!" Anne blurted out, as she picked up the tiny faded paper. She didn't want to lose even a shred of the contents of this collection, so she quickly retrieved the paper.

"I can't read this at all," Anne said. Anne's grandmother had told her each thimble had been a gift from a different person. Details like the year in which the thimble was given, the gifter's name and the thimble's country of origin were all listed on each tiny label.

The weighty collection was comprised of nearly one hundred thimbles, and Anne lifted each one of them to see where to replace the rogue label. "Well, that doesn't' make any sense," Anne said frustrated to find that no thimble was missing a label. Confused, she tucked the loose label into the lining of the case then slid the re-latched case back under her mattress.

On the floor near her feet was a paper folded oddly, as if it had been pressed in a tight space for a long time. "What's this?" Anne said. The first line was visible, "Dear, Anne."

With no delay, Anne unfolded the paper to find a letter.

Dear Anne,

Your aunt Tamara and I were lifelong friends until her passing. Your dear Uncle Royal followed her in death soon after.

She treasured these thimbles and was the third-generation caretaker. One thimble in particular—one made of deep green emerald—was her most prized. She told me once, "At the third watch of night (midnight to three o'clock in the morning), when the moon shines upon this thimble, reflections of moonlight form a message wrapped in a vivid green vine." Your aunt told me this was the message you were supposed to share with the world.

Surely there must be another explanation for this phenomenon— at least, that's what I thought, until the night I saw the thimble glowing in its case. It reminded me of your sister's words, so the next morning, I prepared the collection for shipment to you right away. I took one last look. The emerald thimble was gone!

I am devastated to deliver this case to you without your aunt's favorite piece, but I hope that one day it finds its way back to you.
        Sincerest wishes,
        A friend

Stunned, Anne folded the letter in half and slid it under her mattress where the case was kept.

All evening, Anne pondered everything she had read. The words made her restless. Suddenly, her fear of being taken *out* of the home turned into a fear of being kept *in* the home. As she had done so many times before, Anne collected her things. *I have to get out of here,* she thought.

A glimmer of light caught Anne's eye from outside her window. *Yard cats,* she thought. But, as she looked closer she saw someone out there. Before she could make out the details, a voice from the downstairs called her to dinner.

Anne billowed down the staircase wearing the ruffled blue dress the pastor's wife had provided for her. Dresses always felt strange to Anne. Like a wave of the ocean, the five children rushed by her side and took their usual places at the family table, leaving one vacant chair at each end.

"Well, take your place, Anne." The pastor's wife directed. "Oh, you don't *have* a place. How silly of me."

The pastor's wife turned to her eldest son, "Darling, please add a chair for Anne." In swift motion, he burst through the front door and returned with a wooden chair on his shoulder. Without speaking, he positioned the chair for Anne.

"Thank you," Anne said, batting down the blue fluff of her dress in an attempt to tuck the stubborn cloud of fabric below the table. Minutes later, the pastor entered.

"Welcome home, Jim," Lisa greeted above a chorus of the children's greetings. Jim smiled, as if to prove to the audience that a day of Bible study and visitation of the poor had not thoroughly exhausted him. He detoured to the family sitting area, where he opened his satchel to remove a large family Bible, which he placed on the side table. Then, he made his way to the last vacant chair at the table.

"Let us pray," Jim said.

Anne, with her head bowed low, peeked through the tiny separations of her eyelids to find the youngest family member holding back laughter as the family pup's sloppy tongue tickled his fingers below the table. More than any other time of day, dinnertime reminded Anne that things were different now. No more silent meals across the long dining table from Lady Kathryn. For a moment, she lost herself in thought: *I don't know what life has for me, but things sure are changing.*

"Anne, the potatoes?" the pastor's wife repeated.

"Oh, I'm sorry, Miss Lisa. Here, will you please pass these potatoes to Miss Lisa?" Anne asked the young lad to her left, as she brought her thoughts back into the present.

After dinner, Lisa called Anne into the kitchen where the ruckus of dishes bubbling in buckets of lye soap hindered communication. "Could you run these out to the girl?" Lisa asked.

"Oh, yes, Ma'am. The girl?" Anne answered.

"Yes, the girl, Josey. She's out by the barn." Miss Lisa answered.

Still uncertain, Anne received the plate of scraps from the evening's dinner. "Yes, Ma'am," she said. As she walked out toward the barn, Anne wondered whether the Josey Miss Lisa had sent her to meet could possibly be the same Josey she had just met at the general store. Each step toward the barn introduced a new patch of prickly grass to Anne's bare feet. *That sounds like water,* Anne thought, as she headed in that direction. At the source, she found a young girl, hunched over a wooden barrel.

As Anne walked toward the girl, she saw a beautiful bird perched nearby. Its feathers billowed in the evening breeze as it stood amid the waving flowers that streamed across the landscape. Then, from the corner of her eye, she saw a tiny field mouse scurry through the grass.

"Are you … *Josey?*" Anne asked when she finally reached the girl.

"Yes, Ma'am, I am." Josey answered.

"It *is* you!" Anne exclaimed, recognizing Josey from the general store. "What are you doing out here?"

"Wye, Ma'am, I work here for these good people," Josey answered.

"You work for the pastor?" Anne said. "Then why didn't you join us for dinner?"

"Well, Ma'am—" Josey began.

"Any reason why you are calling me 'Ma'am'?" Anne added.

"Well, Ma'am. Miss Lisa and Mister Jim give me good eating and lodging, and I do their washing up and mending. They've been so good to me," Josey explained.

Anne couldn't believe what she was hearing. Slavery had been outlawed for some years now, being as the Emancipation Proclamation was 1863, and the Thirteenth Amendment to the Constitution removed any doubt of it in 1865. Still, something about this relationship Josey had with Miss Lisa and Pastor Jim felt akin to something Anne did not want to acknowledge.

As Anne stepped closer, Josey stopped scrubbing the wash and moved further inside the barn. She rustled with a few old army uniforms she'd been asked to repair.

"Josey, where are you going?" Anne said as she stepped into the moon-lit barn.

Josey rearranged the uniforms. "Ma'am, I'm taking care not to crease these uniforms," Josey answered, as she secretly slipped something underneath the pile of clothing.

Anne entered slowly, being careful not to invade Josey's territory, and placed the plate of food beside Josey. "Well, here you go," Anne said.

"I thank you, Ma'am," Josey replied.

'The name's Anne," Anne blurted. "I'm not sure we made it that far the other day at the store," Anne said. "Just call me Anne."

Reassured that Anne remembered her, Josey smiled ear to ear. "Thank you, Anne," she said.

"So, what are you doing with all these uniforms?" Anne asked.

"Oh, Miss Lisa gathered these from the soldiers. They all need some mending," Josey answered. "But best not go rummaging," Josey said with urgency, hoping Anne would not disturb the pile and find what she had hidden. "These coats are fragile after all that time in the elements."

Anne, who thought she had seen a glimmer of light among the military coats, quickly released the items. "Oh, of course," Anne said. "I'm sorry."

Josey began eating and bid Anne a goodnight. Anne returned to the main house with her mind full of questions. She remembered the bird and the field mouse. *Josey should have that kind of freedom,* she thought.

Why?

"Why can't slaves be free?" Anne asked pastor Jim.

"Oh, Anne," the pastor began, "slaves *are* free. Josey has no place to go. She's as free as a bluebird, but this is where she chooses to stay."

"In your *barn?!*" Anne reacted without thinking.

"Anne, dear. We're glad to have you here after your dear aunt's passing, but mind that you don't go meddling into matters personal." Pastor Jim said as he stretched out his legs before the fire and reclined his head for a rest. As Anne headed back up the stairs, the pastor reflected on her words.

Later that night, after all were in bed, Anne slipped out the front door and back to the barn where she found Josey doing schoolwork by the light of her lantern. "Hello," Anne whispered.

Josey jumped up, startled, and slammed her book closed.

"I scared you. I'm sorry!" Anne said. "What're you reading?"

"Oh, it's okay. The ladies of the Presbyterian church in town loaned this to me from their little church library—a new book called *Scenes in the Life of Harriet Tubman,*" Josey answered. [NOTE: this actual book printed 1869]

"Harriet Tubman. Didn't she help slaves escape to freedom? The Underground Railroad and all of that, right?" Anne asked.

"Well, I only just started the book," Josey said.

"Josey," Anne said in a sudden change of tone. "Let's get out of here."

"*Now?*" Josey replied.

"*Yes!*" Anne said with excitement. "Well," Anne added, coming back to her senses, "not exactly *now*, but first thing in the morning. Let's see what's out there for us, you and me—besides this old barn."

Josey sat back down and looked around the barn dimly lit with a mix of moonlight and her kerosene lamp. "They've been good to me here," Josey said. "I wouldn't know where to begin."

"I have a plan," Anne responded. "We can pack up tonight. It's probably best if we bury my valuables here in the barn, I think," Anne thought out loud as she strategized.

"Valuables?" Josey asked.

"Well, I have a grand collection of thimbles, and I wouldn't want to lose any more on the journey—one's already gone missing," Anne answered. "They were my Great Grandmother's.

Josey was surprised to learn that Anne was protecting thimbles, too, like the one she treasured secretly among her things in the barn. "Anne, if you think you can make it, I'm willing to join you."

"I know we can," Anne said with confidence. Anne returned to the house and reappeared at the barn minutes later with all of her belongings. "There! Now, just bury this case where you see fit, and we'll be all set to leave in the morning."

Josey shook her head in agreement, and Anne headed back to the main house. *Somehow, I've got to bring that collection with us,* Josey thought. *I have a feeling we're not coming back.*

As Josey tried to sleep, a compulsion to view the thimble collection overtook her. She opened the case, and the beauty of the collection filled her with awe. She saw the empty compartment with only a label and no thimble. *This must be the one Anne said was missing,* Josey thought.

A pit of guilt seized Josey. *Oh, no,* Josey thought, as the realization hit her. *My thimble—the one I found—it belongs in this case.* Josey sat contemplating what to do. *If I tell her I have it, she may not want me on her journey.*

This is the Day

The next morning, Anne heard the sound of clapping. She turned to see her parents and grandparents clapping for her. "God is with you, Anne!" they shouted. Suddenly, Anne awoke to the sound of rain clapping on the rooftop. *What a dream!* Anne thought. *Maybe they really are cheering me on.*

Anne jumped up from her bed, got dressed, grabbed a few rolls for herself and Josey, and headed toward the barn.

"Here, Josey!" Anne said in high spirits as she tossed a roll to Josey who had been mending clothing since dawn. "Today's the day, you know. I'll be back at supper time."

"And who is this little guy?" Anne said bending down to pet a loose cat.

"Oh, that's the reverend's cat. He's always saying a cat that don't catch mice is good for nothing," Josey answered.

"Good for *petting!*" Anne said. "And what's her name?"

"She ain't got one as far as I know," Josey said.

"No *name?*" Anne said, appalled and thrilled. "Then we shall call her Rhea. That means ease and flow—just what we need. The Greek myth says that Rhea put up with poor treatment of her children for too long, but ultimately, she made the right choice. We just learned about this in school." Anne lifted Rhea from the ground and swirled her around the barn. "She's coming with us," Anne said as she jetted back through the rain to the main house. "See you tonight!" She shouted behind her as she ran.

"Well, I guess you will be a good companion, little cat," Josey said. "Or, should I call you Rhea?"

The Journey Begins

As usual, Anne ate supper with the family and took a plate of food to Josey. The mood was unlike any other evening the girls had shared. Neither girl voiced her concerns about the trip—though they both had them.

"The stew is perfect for this wet day, isn't it," Anne said.

"It *is.*" Josey answered.

They stacked the dishes, grabbed their belongings and took off, walking all night until the sun rose behind them. Surrounded by their friendly animal companions, they felt strange comfort.

The girls stopped at a pool of cloudy water along the path. Anne examined it as she pulled it to her mouth. "A little dirt never hurt anything," she said without conviction.

Stories of soldiers swiping up stray dogs and cats for a hot meal swirled around Josey's head. She didn't know if it was true, but she thought they better keep their caravan off the beaten path just in case.

In two days of walking, the girls reached a clearing from which they could see a sign that read Verona Train Station. Anne said, "Josey, this is where we split up."

"Split up?" Josey said. "Is that the plan?"

"Well, it's the start," Anne said. "Your talents will make a way for you in the city. I know they will."

Josey sat down without saying a word. She stared out at the train station and imagined her next steps. "Are you scared, Anne?" Josey asked.

"Scared? I've been through too much to be scared," Anne said indignantly.

"I know you're *brave*, but are you *scared* … of letting me down?" Josey asked.

Anne, looking forward at the station stood silently. "I wasn't sure we would get this far," Anne answered after a few quiet minutes.

Josey stood up and put her arm around Anne. "You know, I am not your responsibility, but I am your friend. I see your heart—that you wanted better for me even if you didn't really know what that would be."

A tear fell from Anne's eye, and her strong expression softened it. "Oh, Josey. Thank you."

The girls grabbed their belongings and headed down the hill to the station where they presented enough money for two tickets to Fort Defiance. Still not knowing what they would do with their pets, they meandered along the platform.

"I think I hear the train," Josey said.

"Yes, I hear it!" Anne said.

As they looked upon the train now in full view, they fell violently to the ground under a pile of warm arms and legs attached to haversacks.

"What were you *thinking!* You could have killed us!" Anne shouted, dusting herself off. "Josey, are you *okay?*"

A wily pair of boys pulled their haversacks off of the girls. "Now you don't have to be mean about it," one of the boys said. "I think you broke our fall pretty well."

"I ought to close one of those big ornery eyes for that comment," Anne said with an intimidating fist in the air.

"Okay, I'm sorry, lady. I'm *sorry!*" the boy said. "Now, shouldn't we make introductions before we go punching each other's lights out?" Billy paused and grasped Rascal's shoulders from behind. "This here is Rascal," the boy said, placing Rascal square in front of himself as a sort of shield.

"Well, the well-respected women to whom you speak are called Josey Jackson and Anne of Berryhill," Anne said with as much of Old Lady Kathryn's indignity as she could muster. "Now, who are *you!*" Anne said, directly at the boy.

Rascal spoke up as he presented his friend, "Wye, this is Billy Washita!"

"Billy Washita," Anne repeated, stepping toward Billy. "Well, it's nice to meet you. Here's something to remember me by." With that, Anne swung her clenched fist right at Billy's face.

"WHOA! Whoa!" Rascal exclaimed.

"I think you blacked my eye," Billy said, holding his right eye.

"Well, it wasn't supposed to be a handshake," Anne said. "Now, maybe you'll remember that eye when you go about disrespecting women."

Billy, still holding his eye stood stunned. Then, Rascal and Josey, as if orchestrated to the very second, simultaneously broke the silence with laughter. The laughter spread to Billy and finally to Anne. Even the pets began jumping and wagging.

"I guess we made intro-ductions, didn't we" Billy sputtered between laughs.

Something about that first meeting sealed the friendship of this unlikely gang.

Ask Yourself

1. Anne was more concerned about her own future than losing Lady Kathryn who had not been a very close relationship. What do you think this response says about Anne's fears?
2. Anne appreciated the hospitality of the pastor, but she challenged him on his treatment of Josey. What does it mean to speak the truth in love?
3. Why do you think Josey hesitated to tell Anne about her glowing thimble?
4. Josey's empathy toward Anne was healing when Anne thought separation from her friend was better than the risk of letting Josey down. Has fear of failure ever caused you to push a person away?

Outdoor Survival Tips: Identify Poisonous Plants

Heed the old saying, "Leaves of three. Let it be." It refers to the three-leaved shaped of poison ivy. Make sure you get acquainted with the appearance and other identifying features of poisonous plants in your area, so you don't end up wishing you had just *let it be.*

Follow Billy's Journey

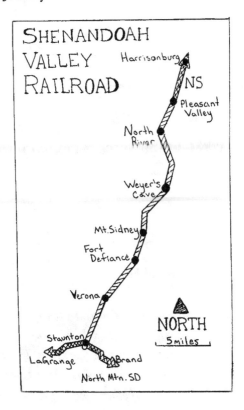

Chapter Five

Fort Defiance, Virginia

Confrontation with General Hunt

Dear Ma and Pa,

As luck would have it, we are now a gang of four, including a couple of runaways named Anne and Josey. Anne says they bring sophistication to our journey, and maybe that's true. The girls rode in their official seats, while Rascal, the animals and I hopped onto the back with a surprising number of others who had the same idea.

We are keeping a low profile in Fort Defiance, since there is no adult in our party. A hidden cottage we stumbled upon by accident works for now. It isn't clean, but it's sturdy. It has two bedrooms on the ground and three in the upper level. From the top, I see a lake between the trees. You always did like a good view.

Rascal and I were excited to find an old horse-drawn wagon and farm tools. Homes have a certain feeling to them, and the feeling in this house is peace and love. Far off, there is an older man who emerges to maintain his property from time to time. We're not sure yet, if we should attempt to meet him.

I wish you were here, Pa. They ask me to say grace each night. I think it gives them comfort, like it comforted me when you prayed. Well, something's working, because I'm writing this by a crackling fire, a few fishing poles and a belly full of wild berries.

I love you,

Billy

A Place to Call Home

Now, in Fort Defiance, the gang was in top spirits having found an abandoned cottage big enough to house them all comfortably. They settled in and established patterns. The boys brought up water daily from a nearby lake, now visible through the bald winter trees, and laid rabbit traps to make up the difference on those days when the fish weren't biting. The girls put up a slight fuss against killing cute little rabbits for a few days until the fish ran low and Billy came in with a fresh roasted supper.

Josey thought if the gang was planning still to be in the cottage in springtime, they better get seeds in the ground. So, as the winter weather lost its chill, she and Anne planted lines of vegetable seeds they found wrapped in cloth in the barn.

The boys explored the neighboring town, Mt. Sidney, to determine if it would be wise for the gang to relocate. With no one really eager to leave yet, the group decided unanimously to remain in the cottage through the spring.

"We need to find some work," Billy said one night over dinner. "We've been here a few months now, and there's no use living off the goods of this old house without putting something into it ourselves."

"Uh hem," Anne interjected. "Those spring greens you're eating didn't plant themselves."

"Right, right. I know that. I'm just thinking about the future," Billy said.

"So, what do you say we do?" Rascal asked, accustomed to following Billy's leadership.

"For now, we best use our mouths for chewing," Billy said shooting a glance toward Anne. "But tomorrow, let's scout it out. "

The next morning, the boys packed up a few supplies and started walking. They came across a field of the first summer watermelons. The field extended a long way leading to a humble little cabin.

Hungry from their trek, Billy said, "What do you think about a nice sweet snack?"

"A watermelon?" Rascal said.

"Of course, a watermelon. They need testing, don't they?" Billy said.

"I suppose they do," Rascal said, catching on.

They boys laughed as they stepped closer to the watermelon patch. But, as they came within feet of delicious looking new watermelons, they suddenly felt rather conspicuous.

"Do you think they can see us from that cabin?" Rascal asked.

"Look here, Rascal. You're too far back. When you step into the patch a bit those trees completely block us," Billy said, gesturing Rascal to join him. "They won't see a thing. It's like stealing a slice of pie from grandma's window."

"Stealing? Now, we're not stealing … we're testing," Rascal said, trying to ease his conscience.

"Right. We're testing. Let's get to it!" Billy said. "Hey, where's that knife of yours anyway?"

As Rascal reached for the knife, somehow, he couldn't find it in his haversack. He pulled the bag back to get a glimpse of it, but each time he inserted his hand to feel around for the sheath, it seemed to disappear.

Tired of waiting, Billy said, "Forget the knife, I have a better idea. If we just bash a dozen or so, the farmer will just think a pack of coyotes stopped in for a snack," Billy said, hungry and proud. "And, that way, we can get right to the heart of the melon—the sweetest part!"

As Billy's excitement grew, Rascal's diminished, partly from disappointment over not being able to find his knife when he needed it. But, before Rascal could agree, *SMASH!* A watermelon twice the size of a cannon ball exploded on a nearby rock.

"This is amazing!" Billy said with a mouthful of bright red fruit. "Here, have one!"

Instinctively, Rascal caught the watermelon then tossed it against a stone on the ground. "Wow, you're not kidding. I could eat a hundred of these," Rascal said.

"A *thousand,*" Billy answered.

By the end, the boys had eaten the heart out of about four watermelons each.

A Soldier's Agreement

"Can stomachs burst?" Rascal said, holding his abdomen.

"I know what you mean," Billy answered. "Those girls will lose their lids if they find out we stuffed ourselves all morning. Let's keep this between you, me and these half-dozen watermelon rinds."

"We should probably be going," Rascal said, as he rolled to his feet. The boys waddled back toward the wagon.

"Young soldiers!" a voice called out.

The boys froze. "Oh, no!" Billy whispered in Rascal's direction.

"Oh, no," Rascal whispered—but for an altogether different reason. He wasn't sure he could make it another second without wetting his pants on account of all of those watermelons. When the boys turned around, they saw a man of impressive stature with a patch over one eye and a peg for a leg. The man wore a perfectly white undershirt and pristinely clean military-issue pants.

The man approached the boys. "Well, looks like we have a couple of turncoats in our midst," he said. The boys didn't answer. "So, tell me, young men, what would you do in my situation?" The boys remained silent. "Now, at least give me the dignity of an answer. You do know how to speak like men, do you not?"

Rascal, a leader when necessary, spoke up: "(gulp) Sir …"

"Now, you stop right there, young man. You may call me General Hunt," the man said.

"Yes, Sir. General Hunt, Sir, we're sorry for eating your watermelon without permission," Rascal said.

General Hunt's good eye darted between the two boys, as if measuring their sincerity. "Boys, you are forgiven, but I must say, my darling Joanna is not yet home from town. She won't be pleased, as her sweat is represented in this field, as well she'll have her own two cents, but it will go better for you if we agree on remunerations," he said.

"Remuner*whats?*" Billy said.

"Son, your actions cost me the price of these watermelons, and you're going to make up that cost. That's remuneration," the general explained. "Now, I'll pay you a small sum, and you'll plow my fields. That will remind you of the work that goes into each fruit and vegetable. How is 25 cents per day?"

Relieved at the general's graciousness, Billy and Rascal jumped at the offer. "Sir, yes, sir!" they said. "Yes, sir, indeed."

"Good, then," the general answered. "In that case, I'll work up a soldier's agreement for our mutual signatures. I'll just need your names."

"My name is Rascal," Rascal said promptly.

"And, my name is Billy *Vo*—… *err*, Billy *Washita!*" Billy said with a fumble.

"You don't know your own name, son?" the general asked.

"Sure, he does. He's just getting used to it!" Rascal exclaimed, followed by an *"OWE!"* when Billy threw a slight elbow to the ribs.

"General Hunt, my name took a beating back at home, so I figured it was better all the way around to start fresh," Billy explained.

"A sullied name, huh?" the general said. "Well, you're right that names have power, but you may find that a name worth having is a name worth redeeming."

"Yes, sir," Billy said, rather confused.

"Now, Billy Vaw, just sign your name right here," the general said with a gesture to a few lines of agreement he'd scratched into the paper of his leather-bound notebook.

"It's *Vogt*, Sir," Billy corrected.

"Vogt, you say?" the general said.

"Yes … Sir," Bill said. *If this is the same General Hunt who led my father in battle, I hope he never knows I'm the son of his soldier. My father would be so ashamed if he knew I'd stolen,* Billy thought, relieved that the general didn't seem to make the connection.

After all the names had been signed, the general spoke: "Rascal, you are a young man of promise. Wield your sword for what is right. One day, you will slay a giant of generations with no fear in your heart. You have a mind to build sturdy structures, and your creativity will change the world. The world waits for you to claim your rightful place as an innovator—not to steal watermelon from old men."

Then, the general turned to Billy and said, "Billy, your father fought nobly in the war under my direction. He left behind his most dear treasures on earth in the fight for freedom: the love of his life, your mother, and his dear twins. I knew one day I would meet you, because the Lord gave me a message for you. For years, I've carried it."

The general pulled a folded paper from his pants pocket. As he unfolded it, Billy could make out stamped letters spelling out CONTINENTAL ARMY. The general began reading:

Now, is the time for you to lay down your gun and let peace rule your heart. Lead an army without malice, pain and fear. I have removed the strongholds, so you may assemble your troops for a new and greater plan.

You no longer are an orphan but a true son. Your life will save those whose lives have been rampaged by a war that has taken their parents. Those, you will lead as part of your family and bring them into the city without shame.

As you abide in me, the Lord Christ, you will build new communities. You will assemble workers to accomplish this end.

I have seen your struggle as you survive in your own power. Now, rest in my strength. Lean on me, and I will bring you to a pleasant valley overflowing with peace, joy and wealth greater than money.

Your pen will write the truth of God. Your lineage will thrive, and your story will ripple throughout the world, as you proclaim the life and return of Christ.

Billy, struck with silence, felt at once known yet foreign to his own understanding of himself. *General Hunt actually knew my Pa!* He thought. The excitement stirred in equal parts with a humbling sense that the Almighty God—the one his father spoke of with such conviction—actually saw him and knew him intimately. There were no words for that.

"And, you, Rascal. I'll see you tomorrow, bright and early, ready to work," the general said. "And be prepared to stay for dinner," the general said, now addressing both boys. "I'm not sure what my dear Joanna will say to you, but I'm sure she'll want to do it over a warm meal."

With that, the boys made their way to the wagon and returned to the cottage, Rascal said, "Say, Rascal. Did you hear that bit about twins?"

"I did," Billy said. "Best I can guess is that a message gets mixed up after all these years." The aroma of vegetable porridge swooned the boys as they approached the girls.

"We have to tell them, don't we," Rascal said.

"Do we?" Billy said.

"You know we do," Rascal said with a smile.

The gang gathered around the table for a satisfying meal, and Rascal recounted their encounter at the watermelon patch. Anne erupted in fury to hear of their exploits but softened when she learned of their new wage-earning positions.

Early the next morning, the boys loaded the wagon for their first day on the job. Joanna met them at the door with biscuits and bacon, but the hospitality stopped there. "Gentlemen, I've heard of your deeds, and I'm deeply disturbed by this criminality."

Uh oh, the boys thought.

"But, as the General has seen fit to pardon you, I, too, expunge your offenses against us and our property," she said. "The General is working the northeast corner of the field. I suggest you get down there and start working."

With mouths still full of biscuits, the boys hustled to find the general. They located him among a quarter-mile of tomatoes and squash. "Wow!" Billy said.

"Young men," the general said. Something about the title "young men" always made Rascal and Billy stand up a bit taller. "Hear this: Whatever is right in the Lord's sight with a pure heart." He continued, "Whether one wins a war or finds the love of a good women, he will find himself baffled with dissatisfaction without the Lord's companionship. But, when men do what's right in the Lord's sight, darkness and death flee their hearts. With soft hearts, they are eager to do God's work on the earth."

The general wiped sweat from his brow. "Now, give me five rows plowed by the time the sun hits that oak tree there. You see the one?"

The boys nodded their heads nervously in affirmation.

"Good," the general said. "When you finish, report back to the house for a hot meal," he said.

The boys gazed on the impossible task and got to work. General Hunt turned toward the house, bent down to clutch a handful of dirt for examination, then hobbled back toward the house as he sprinkled the dirt to the wind.

As the boys neared the oak tree toward the end of their day's work, they were pleasantly surprised to find a pale of clean water waiting for them under the shade of the tree. They alternated long swigs as they returned to the house. Soon, their interest in water turned to a nose to the air, as the smell of lamb stew wooed them through the last quarter mile.

"Smell that, Rascal?" Billy said.

"Smells like Heaven!" Rascal answered.

"Smells like … *cornbread!* Did we hit the jackpot or what?" Billy said. "C'mon! Supper's waitin'!"

When the boys reached the house, the table was set with two large baskets and a large black pot suspended over a small open fire. The general led the table in prayer and began passing items to the left.

"Scone?" the general said, as he handed one of the large baskets to Billy.

"Thank you, General." Billy said. He placed one scone on his plate and tucked a second one between his legs.

"Scone, Rascal?" Billy said to Rascal, as he shot him an instructive wink and gestured to the extra scone in his lap.

"Ohhhhh, a *SCONE!*" Rascal responded, winking awkwardly at Billy. Rascal never was one for subtlety.

Catching onto the boys' scheme, the general said, "Now, didn't we talk about stealing, young men?"

"Oh, we're not stealing. Really," Billy said.

"No, we're really not. We're … *appreciating!*" Rascal added.

"The hardworking boys I know learned their lesson and aren't the type to go about appreciating other peoples' things without good cause. So, what's going on here that you would take extra food when my Joanna here has offered you a table full of more than you could possibly enjoy?" the general asked.

Billy answered, "You see, General, you're right. There is more here than we could possibly enjoy. And, we *are* grateful. Aren't we grateful, Rascal?

Rascal nodded his head and said, "Oh, boy *are we!* We haven't had food this good since … well, maybe the town potluck a few summers back."

Billy continued, "But, see, the food we put back isn't for *our* bellies."

"We have women at home," Rascal blurted out.

"Women, you say?" the general said.

"More like *sisters*—" Billy said, shooting another baffled glance at Rascal. "… Josey and Anne. And, yes. They're home eating fresh greens and the first of the apple crop, but they sure would do anything for a taste of this blueberry scone, General … um, *Sir,*" Billy said.

"Well, why didn't you say anything before now!" Joanna said suddenly. "You bring them here tomorrow, and we'll find work. Between the cabin and this garden, there's plenty for a few extra sets of hands."

"Yes," the general agreed. "You can let those girls ride on that wagon you're pulling. You think a horse might make the road a bit easier?"

For the first time since meeting the general, the boys laughed. For months, they'd been the horse for their own wagon, and they realized how ridiculous that must look. "A horse would put us to shame, alright," Rascal said, laughing.

"Why don't you boys help Mrs. Joanna here with the washing up, and I'll get my horse ready for you," the general said.

The next night, the entire gang joined the general and his wife for another hot supper. Gratitude, kind words and genuine appreciation for the other people warmed the room unlike the gang had experienced since launching their journey.

"Anne," Billy said. "The general was telling us last night how to reach the trail head of Mount Sidney. That will put us on a fine track to reach our destination."

"Really?" Anne said with a smile.

"Aren't you feeling hungry, my darling?" the general said to Joanna.

Startled, she answered, "Oh, silly me. I suppose I got lost for a moment there. General, how did we stumble upon such fine children."

Joanne's unusual softness brought silence to the table. "They are fine children, yes." the general said.

For 24 days, the gang worked the farm—with the girls taking every other day off to see to the needs of their own cottage in the woods.

"I count $18 dollars here, Billy," Rascal said, one day on the ride back to the cottage. "That's more than enough for four tickets to Harrisonburg!"

Billy was quiet. "Yeah, I figured wages were adding up pretty good," he answered. "I guess we best keep our next steps quiet around the general, so he doesn't go alerting a bunch of adults to come see to our care."

"You think he would do that?" Rascal asked.

"It's too risky to think otherwise. We've come too far. And, those girls better keep their traps locked, too," Billy said. His tone harshened like it always did when he thought about things that scared him. Not knowing all the answers just happened to be one of those things.

The next evening, after dinner, General Hunt brought the children in the living room for tea and said, "Children, you bring light to our home, and I know I speak for Joanna when I say that although we have been honored to bless you with wages, meals and lessons of life, you have blessed us all the more."

Rascal looked at Billy to see if the plan had changed or whether they were still agreed to keep their mouths shut about their departure. One sharp glance from Billy removed all doubt—Rascal's lips were sealed.

Maybe General Hunt had a feeling the gang was ready for the next chapter of their journey, because his words sounded like a farewell speech: "Billy, I've told you your father was a hero. He shielded more than a dozen men on the battle field. Do you know from where a man summons that kind of courage?" The general handed Billy a large dusty package wrapped in fabric and tied with a green ribbon. Billy opened it to find a leather-bound book.

"A Bible," Billy said.

"This Bible belonged to your great grandfather," the general said.

Billy carefully lifted the cover and found two lines of text inscribed

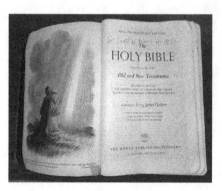

TRAIL OF TEARS, 1830 GREAT IS OUR GOD—II CHRONICLES 2:5

Remembering how to locate verses from the childhood instruction he'd received from the ladies at his church, Billy placed his thumb directly in the middle of the thick stack of Bible pages and allowed about one quarter of those pages to fall below his thumb until the book revealed II Chronicles.

Billy read aloud beginning at chapter two and verse five: "And the house which I build is great: for great is our God above all gods."

Billy looked up, "But, what does it mean?"

"Billy, I trust you will know as you go," the general said. Now, Billy was certain someone had squealed of their plan to continue their journey and not very pleased about it. "You will do even greater things than your father but in peace not war. You will plant churches. And, the time is here to put away deceptive justifications and false statements, which are displeasing to God."

Billy felt entirely seen.

Josey looked at Anne with concern. *"I don't know how Billy takes to being told what to do,"* she thought.

The gang thanked the Hunts and said goodbye for the evening. They pulled their wagon to the edge of the trail alongside a small pond and decided to catch a few fish. The boys always caught more fish in the dark.

"That got a little rough back there," Anne said to Billy.

"Oh, what? The general?" Billy said, casting his line to the middle of the pond. "Nah. His words are good enough for my Pa; they're good enough for me. My Pa loved that man, and I think—" Billy stopped abruptly.

"Okay, Billy," Anne said. *Wow,* she thought. *That is not the Billy I know. What in the world happened to him?* Anne was shocked but relieved to hear Billy's gentle demeanor. She shared with Josey about their short exchange, and Josey couldn't believe it.

"What?!" Josey said. "You mean he actually listened to General Hunt? What is going on here?"

The gang settled near each other in the same grassy patch near the pond's edge and chatted between catches.

"Another one!" Rascal shouted. "That makes *13!* What is it—a full moon or something?"

The boys strung up another catfish on their line. Then, they heard an ear-piercing shriek. They turned to see Anne covering Josey's mouth from behind. Anne looked directly at the boys. She put one finger over her own mouth to instruct them to be silent. Then, she pointed across the pond.

On the other side of the pond, 14 sparkling blue eyes looked back at the gang. A howl erupted.

"Chupacabra!" Josey screamed, pulling Anne's hand down from her mouth momentarily.

"Oh, there's no such thing!" Billy said, dismissively. "That's all legend. It's just a bunch of coyotes."

"Do coyotes look like bald bears? Because those don't look like any coyotes I've ever seen. My dad told me they drink blood," Josey responded, again pulling Anne's hand down just long enough to speak then replacing it like a shield.

"While you guys argue this out, I'm getting out of here," Anne said. She pulled her hand from Josey's mouth, grabbed her fishing pole and headed toward the wagon. "C'mon Rascal!" she said.

"Grab this!" Rascal yelled back, holding out one side of a string of catfish.

All four grabbed their supplies and jumped in the wagon. They took off as fast as their horse could run and didn't say a word until they reached the cottage.

"So," Anne said cautiously. "What *was* that?"

"Chupacaaaaabra." Billy said in a mocking tone.

Just then, Rascal, who was unloading the fish, spoke up. "What *happened* here?" he said. "They're *gone!*"

"It's all HEADS!" Billy shouted, lifting up the other end of the fishing line. "What happened to the *bodies?*"

"You mean something *ate the fish,"* Anne exclaimed, "and we didn't even see it?!" She jumped from the wagon and ran inside. "What is *happening?*"

"They were Chupa—Well, you know," Josey said, following Anne to the cottage.

The gang rushed inside—first Anne, then Josey, followed by Billy, then Rascal. Just as he stepped up to the porch, a light caught Rascal's eye. He looked down to see a glow coming from the sheath attached to his belt.

"You go ahead," Rascal called." He grasped his knife and ran toward the trees next to the cottage. With a few swift strokes, he sliced thick branches with surprising ease. In seconds, his arms were full of sturdy branches. He returned to the porch and stacked them against the front door as he closed himself into the cottage. The sound of wild beasts filled the garden near the house. By the light of his knife, he could see them ravage the field of all of its produce.

Rascal ran upstairs to find the other three huddled in the back of the room. "So, the fish are gone. I reckon the garden is gone, too. Does anyone think maybe tomorrow's the day to get out of here?" he said.

"We're good as gone!" Billy said.

Ask Yourself

1. Billy and Rascal said they were just *testing* the watermelons *What's the big deal about taking a few watermelons when no one's looking?*

2. When Billy got caught stealing, why do you think he didn't want General Hunt to know he was the son of Alan Vogt?

3. It can be hard to take instruction from someone when you don't believe the person cares for you. Why do you think Billy took General Hunt's correction so easily?

4. The gang and General and Mrs. Hunt grew to enjoy each other. So, why do you think the orphans planned to leave town secretly?

5. Billy didn't know what to think about the messages in his great grandfather's Bible. What can you do when you find a verse in the Bible that doesn't make sense?

Outdoor Survival Tips: Account for Sunlight

On the earth's one-year track around the sun, it makes about 365 revolutions (You know these as *days!*). Because the earth revolves on a tilted axis, the earth receives different exposure to the sun based on its position on the one-year track. For example, during winter, a 24-hour day has less sunlight, but in summer, sunlight begins earlier and lasts longer. Consider the amount of usable sunlight you'll have (the time between sunrise and sunset) as you plan your journey. And, remember—the sun rises in the east and sets in the west.

Follow Billy's Journey

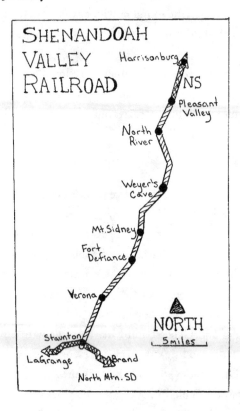

Chapter Six

Mt. Sidney, Virginia

Can I Change My Name?

Dear Ma and Pa,

I was thinking about names. Even names with no proper definition still reveal something—a lineage, a story, lives lived, loved ones remembered. Every name has a story to tell.

We made a new friend. He picked up the name "Chubby" growing up, so he's been thinking about names, too, I suppose. He's been asking what we would name him if we could change his name. Personally, I think we need to know a person, and let the name make itself. But, I can see why he's in a rush. You would have a good name for him, Pa. Was it you who named me?

It's unnerving, people depending on me. You never let fear lead you (II Timothy 1:7), you used to say, but every time I reach for wisdom, fear seems to come creeping in.

Our next stop is Mount Sidney. I'm hoping we'll find trails in those mountains and that one of those trails leads us to Harrisonburg.

If not, we're sunk—but there goes fear again. Say a prayer for me, will you?

I'm surprised I'm saying this, but our gang would match up against any gang I could have assembled—girly girls and all. Around the campfire, when we're sharing stories, we all seem pretty much alike. I guess orphans know a thing or two about orphans.

I sure can't wait to find Aunt Sunny.

Love you,

Billy

To Mount Sidney

"What a night?!" Billy said, yawning. "My achin' neck!"

"You can sleep on the ground, but your neck can't handle one night on the floor?" Anne said.

"Alright, alright. Let's just get our belongings in the wagon. This map shows about a two days' journey to Mount Sidney," Billy said with confidence.

"I think I'll miss Fort Defiance," Josey said, "Chupacabra or not."

"They were *coyotes*," Billy muttered. *I just don't know why there would not be one single BEWARE COYOTES sign in all of Fort Defiance,* he pondered. He'd learned on his journey to let go of the things he simply didn't understand.

With a wagon packed with people, poles and what remained of their food, they took off on a gentle wagon trail out of town. "I'd say we have a solid week of food if we ration properly," Billy told the gang. "We have five full canteens, but keep an eye out for water, as we go. We'll want to collect any clean water we find."

All day they traveled, stopping once to water the horse. They stopped to camp in an area that seemed to be somewhat frequented by people. *We must be getting close to town if there's evidence of people coming through here not too long ago,* Billy thought. Billy hoped to find an elevated landing from which to look down on Mount Sidney before they entered the town. The height would give him a good view of the train into town (to see if the crew could easily stowaway on it).

"I don't understand why we couldn't just take the train into Harrisonburg," Rascal said.

"Don't you know anything, Rascal?" Billy said. "We're runaways. And, Josey. What if she's caught? Do you think anyone will appreciate ungrateful runaways if we get sent back? The more people we see, the higher the chances we're caught."

Billy continued, "When we get to Pleasant Valley, I'm thinking we'll be safe to hop the train for that last leg into Harrisonburg."

"And, how far is Pleasant Valley?" Anne asked.

"We have bigger things to worry about than distance," Billy said.

"What do you mean by that?" said Rascal.

"Nothin'," Billy answered.

"Billy, what do you see on that map of yours?" Anne demanded. She took the map and rotated it two, three, four times. "How do you work this thing?"

"Gimme that," Billy said, retrieving his map. "If you must know, we have a hike coming up."

"Isn't that what we've *been* doing?" Anne asked.

"… and a cave," Billy continued.

"A cave?" Rascal echoed.

"… and the North River," Billy said.

"A *RIVER?!*" Anne said.

"You *asked!*" Billy responded.

Billy saw that the news flustered the gang. Even Josey looked concerned about the river, although she didn't mention it. Josey tended to keep her fears to herself, but that didn't mean they weren't real. And, Billy felt responsible to bring peace back to the journey.

"Now, listen, guys. We can do this. A cave is nothing but a big sturdy shelter. That's what we want. And, a river ride will be a welcome departure from this bumpy wagon anyway," Billy said.

"A ride? How do you suggest we *ride* the river? You have a boat?" Anne said.

Billy wasn't sure what to say, but he wasn't going to let fear creep into his leadership. He remembered something the general had said back at the farm. "You'll know as you go," Billy said with a smile. That seemed to settle everyone down—even Billy.

Camp

"Rascal, you really saved us with those branches last night," Billy said. "I don't know what it is with you and that knife, but I'm glad you keep it around."

As the gang setup camp for the night, they began talking about the unique gifts each of them brought to the group. "Anne sure got us out of trouble with those beasts, didn't she?" Rascal said, as he leaned branches to create a lean-to shelter for the night.

From the wagon, where the girls were setting up their beds for the night, about thirty yards from the boys' shelter, Anne answered, "Thank you, Rascal! How about you boys handle security tonight, so we can get some sleep?"

"Billy and Rascal at your service, Madame," Rascal called. Thirty yards was a good distance off—far enough for privacy but close enough to keep watch and chase off any unwanted visitors.

The starlight shining through the lean-to shelter reminded the boys of the first leg of their journey—before they met Anne and Josey. "Say, Billy. Did you hear that shot?" Rascal asked.

"That's gunfire, alright," Billy said. "Nothing to worry about."

"You don't think so?" Rascal asked, still a little gun shy from all the war stories of the recent past.

"The war is over, Rasc. Go to sleep, pal," Billy said. *Poor kid. I had a hard-enough time during the war when my family was helping me understand what was going on. I wonder who helped Rascal understand the war. Maybe no one did?*

Two Options

"Now that's what I call sleep," Anne stated, arms outstretched to the sky, bright and early the next morning. "Oh, did I wake you," Anne said sarcastically in the direction of the lean-to shelter.

"Who you talking to, Anne?" Billy said, walking up with Rascal from behind Anne.

"WYE! Where did *you* come from, Billy Washita?" Anne said, trying to cover the fact that she was startled nearly to death.

Billy smiled. "I think we got her," he said in Rascal's direction. Rascal nodded with a smirk out of Anne's line of sight. Rascal was good about staying on people's good sides if he could help it.

"Well, since you're up," Billy said. "The way I see it we have two options—wagon trail or discreet hiking trail."

"Why would we hike when we can ride?" Anne said.

"We can ride, alright. So, can the rest of Pleasant Valley. And, what do you expect they'll do when they see us four commanding our own wagon?" Billy said.

"Oh," Anne said.

"They'll send us to one of those overcrowded orphanages for children of the war. That's what they'll do," Billy said in a reckless tone.

"So, I guess we're hiking," Anne said.

"But what about the horse?" Josey asked, climbing down from the wagon and walking to pat the horse's mane.

No one had a good answer—or not one that anyone was willing to state out loud anyway, so they let the conversation fade into the distance as they cleaned up for the day. That night, Rascal led the discussion. "You know, each of you remembers something about your parents—not me. I have been in that orphanage since I was a baby—maybe even since the very day of my birth. It wasn't customary for Rascal to refer to the orphanage as "orphanage," so Billy paid particularly close attention to his friend's words.

Rascal continued, "The only memory I have is a dumb box of sundry items the orphanage gave me when I was about seven."

"What's in it?" Josey asked.

"It had a picture of my parents and my mom's thimble was in there, at least I guess it was hers." Rascal said.

There was a rolled-up paper with sketches of a cabin—the kind of sketches that tell you exactly how to build it."

"Like a plan …" Billy added.

"Yeah, like a building plan," Rascal said.

"What a special box," Josey said.

"There was one more thing," Rascal said, making circles in the dirt with his shoe. His left hand rested on Rex's head as he continued, "A letter—to my mother … from my father. He said he loved her and that he loved the children. So, that's something, *right?*"

At that, Rascal tucked his head in his hands. He'd gained so much courage on this journey, he didn't want to look weak now. He wondered if maybe everyone would step away, now that he'd lost his composure, but as he peeked through his fingers, he saw that the other three had moved in closer to him. They flanked him—one on each side and Billy standing just behind him. Billy placed his hand down onto Rascal's shoulder. *Is this what family feels like?* Rascal wondered.

A little later Anne pulled Rascal aside. "So, I suppose your dad was a carpenter among other things, Rascal."

"Wow. And, do you still have that picture?" she asked.

Rascal reached into his shirt pocket. "Be careful not to bend it," he said, as he handed it over.

"They are such a joyful couple, your parents," Anne said before handing the image back to Rascal.

"Thanks," Rascal said.

About the Horse

The next morning, the girls woke up before the boys and took a little walk around camp. As was her custom, Josey meandered over to pet the horse.

"She's GONE!" Josey yelled. "Someone stole her!"

The boys jumped out of the lean-to with such force, that all the sticks that composed the shelter fell to the ground. They tripped over their feet while they ran in the direction of Josey's voice. They were still waking up.

"Where's *Anne?!*" Billy yelled.

Crying, Josey said, "It's not Anne. It's the horse. She's gone."

"Oh, Josey." Billy said. "You nearly killed me. The horse is fine—better than fine. I took her out for a walk last night and found a farm with an extra stall. It was like it was meant to be. Now, she'll be well taken care of while we take this leg on foot."

"You did *what?!*" the others said.

"I had to do it. I was going to tell you," Billy said. "I didn't expect we'd wake up to a robbery!"

"Well, I don't see why not—you robbed us," Anne said, comforting Josey at the head of the wagon.

"We still got these little fellas," Billy said, gesturing to Rex, Ginny and Rhea who had become a faithful and steady presence for the group.

"Until you go giving them away," Anne said, crawling back into the wagon.

"Now, let's move this wagon against this tree. If we need it later, we'll backtrack," Billy said. "No time to waste. Grab your bags, and let's go."

Being on foot again felt a bit uneasy. Every small sound caused the group to pause and check the brush. The terrain grew tougher as they scaled Mount Sidney. "Look at that hawk!" Rascal yelled. He pointed to a low-flying red-tailed hawk. Rhea the cat paid close attention as the hawk dove swiftly down, snatched up a mouse in its beak and jetted straight up and away.

Further down the path, Billy saw something slither across the path into a puddle of water. "Good Lord, did you see that?" Billy said. Rascal hadn't seen it. He'd sensed a warmth coming from his sheathed knife again, and he looked down to find it glowing. "It was a snake, I think."

Rascal's hesitancy turned to boldness. He grabbed the knife and followed where Billy had indicated the snake had traveled. For a moment, Rascal disappeared into dense trees. Then, he emerged with the head of a snake.

"It *was* a snake. RASCAL! That's a Northern Copperhead. It could have killed you!" Billy exclaimed, patting Rascal on the back like Rascal imagined his father would have done.

"It could have killed anyone of us," Rascal said. Then, he carefully buried the snake head and tucked his knife back in its sheath.

Having missed all the excitement, Josey, distracted by the landscape said, "Say, guys. Does anyone else feel like we've been walking up someone's path?"

"You call this a path?" Billy asked.

"Well, I'm not much of a hiker, but, yeah. It looks like it used to be someone's path under all this brush that has grown up," Josey said. "Do you think someone lives up here?"

Billy answered, "I think you're—"

"BILLY!" they all yelled, as Billy plummeted through a blanket of sticks and into a dark hole.

"THUMP!" they heard.

"Oooouuch," Billy moaned.

"Are you okay, Billy?" Rascal yelled down the hole.

"I wouldn't say that," Billy answered.

"Well, at least he didn't break his sense of humor," Anne said, rummaging around her haversack. "Here, toss him this."

Anne launched a loop of heavy rope to Rascal. "Tie a few knots in one end and send the rest to Billy to loop his foot into," Anne said. "Then, get ready to pull."

Rascal, Anne and Josey stood gripping the rope at the knots and waiting for Billy to yell up the signal. "OKAY, PULL!" Billy yelled.

"It's not budging," Rascal said. "How do we lift him straight up an eight-foot cliff?"

"Not so fast, there, bandits," a voice called from further up the mountain. "What are you doing on my land?"

"Who says this is your land," Anne answered, hoping her intensity would intimidate someone who might be trying to defraud them into thinking they had trespassed. "Can't you see your trap has injured our friend. Now, get over and pull!" Anne said, sensing insecurity in the voice's demeanor.

A person emerged from the bushes. "The name's Fredek. Fredek August, but you can call me Chubby."

"Can I call you *strong*, Chubby! because that's what we need right about now—a boy who can pull."

Fredek grabbed hold of the rope. "One, two, PULLLLLL," he chanted. The rope cut into the soft ground surrounding the pit as Billy rose to the surface.

"Hey, thanks, man!" Billy said, extending his hand to Fredek.

"Chubby here is the one who put you in that hole, you know," Anne said, re-looping her rope and returning it to her bag.

"And, he's the one who got me out," Billy said. He turned to Fredek, "You know, I respect a good trap. How long did it take you to make that?"

"You like that?" Fredek said, surprised. "Follow me. I'll show you my kingdom." Fredek was the son of an architect, and he'd inherited a vision for construction.

"Did you hear that, Rascal? Chubby has a kingdom?" Billy laughed. "If I had some crutches, I might consider a trek up that hill to see it."

Rascal used his knife to fashion a set of crutches from the sticks used to cover the trap. "Crutches, you say?" Rascal said, as he tossed the perfect pair of crutches toward the two boys. "Hand those to Billy, Chubbs."

"Rascal, you're too much." Billy said, admiring Rascal's quick handiwork. "These are incredible! Well?" Billy said, turning to Chubby, "What are we waiting for? Take us to your kingdom!"

Anne, who had been acting especially tough lately caught up with Billy as he hobbled up the mountain. "Need any help, Billy?" He shook his head with a smile. "You know, Billy. I'm sorry I clocked you when we first met."

"Oh, maybe I deserved it," Billy said.

"You did," Anne said with a smile. "But, I just wanted to tell you that before you go off dying in a hole somewhere.

"I'm glad you did," Billy said.

At the top of the hill stood three spectacular trees. "What are these?" Josey asked.

"These are Magnolia Acuminata!" Fredek said with pride. "Cucumber trees!"

"Well, why didn't you say that?" Anne said.

"The first cucumber tree was planted in the early 1700s. General Robert E. Lee used one of these as his headquarters, in fact, during the siege of Petersburg."

"Wait a second, is that a house up there?" Rascal said, squinting into the air.

"This is where you'll be staying," Fredek answered. Each tree was equipped with a separate tree house. "Don't worry about hot days or cool nights. These walls are padded with cotton seeds to keep you nice and temperate any time of day. I spent all winter in these and hardly felt a chill."

A sturdy ladder on the middle tree led to the little home above. Each house had two built-in beds. Between the three houses, there were enough beds for the whole gang—plus one leftover for the pets.

Night came, and the gang was glad they followed their newfound stranger into his kingdom. From Josey's treehouse, she could see the gang's new friend out on the balcony of his treetop home. "What're you doing over there, Fredek?" Josey was the only one who refused to use Fredek's nickname. She had a feeling he didn't much like it.

"It's a telescope—a way to see the stars," Fredek called.

"And, what are they doing?" Josey asked.

"They're dancing, like they always do," Fredek answered, peering through his telescope.

"What an interesting fellow, that Fredek," Josey said to Anne as she stepped back into their treehouse.

Who Is this Fredek?

From the third tree to the middle one where Fredek stayed, Rascal called out: "So, how'd you end up here anyway?" The girls instantly quieted their conversation, so they could hear Fredek's answer.

"It's not all *that* complicated, really," Fredek answered. "I was big for my age, so I fixed my birth certificate to verify that I was 16 years of age. That way the army would take me."

"What?" Anne yelled from the other tree, exposing that the girls had been eavesdropping. "Why would you want to go and do a thing like that? *War?*"

Fredek laughed, "I guess there are no private stories when you're yelling them from the treetops."

"You calling us *snoops?*" Anne yelled. "If it weren't for all the chatter, we'd be sleeping by now."

He smiled and turned to face the woods directly in front of his treehouse to allow people in both trees to get a clear earshot of his story. "You see, my Ma couldn't take it anymore with my Pa's drinking and carrying on. He was always yelling at her. I'm pretty sure he hit her when I wasn't around. I didn't see him do it, but I saw the bruises the next day—the whole town saw. One morning, I woke up, and she was gone—and my siblings with her."

"You mean she just left you there?" Anne shouted, practically leaning over her treetop balcony at this point.

"She did," Fredek said. "But, I don't blame her. Sometimes I wonder if she worried about feeding me. I ate too much; I know I did. But I woulda gone hungry if she'd given me the choice. I really—"

Billy, empathizing with Fredek's hidden questions, interrupted Fredek, "Fella, it's no use blaming yourself or trying to know things you just can't know. Besides," Billy said waving his arms to point out the three magnificent tree homes, "she must've known you'd have your own kingdom someday."

"Yeah, you're right." Fredek said, calmer now. "I figure she had all she could handle with the little ones, and she must have thought I could make it on my own. I thought I could, too, actually, but when Ma was gone, Pa turned out his anger on me. It wasn't more than a month before I realized I had to get out of there."

"So, you have siblings out there," Billy said.

"I do! ... *Did* ... Do," Fredek said. The enthusiastic new friend slowly deflated, like a man staring into a river remembering the day his horse died. "I haven't thought about them in a good while. They settled in Harrisonburg according to a letter I intercepted right before I ran away. When I read that they were safe, I suppose I kind of put them in God's hands."

"Chubby!" Rascal shouted. "Billy!" he shouted again, as if connecting the dots in real time. "HEY!" Rascal said excitedly, shifting his glance between Fredek and Billy. "*WE* are going to Harrisonburg!" The gang remained quiet. Rascal wasn't sure if he'd said something wrong.

"You should come with us," Anne yelled from her balcony.

"Really?" Fredek said. His eyes brightened.

"Heck, why *not*!" Billy agreed after a few moments of deliberation. "You can *build*. We know you can *trap*, and now we know you're a regular *soldier*. Say, what was the worst thing you saw in the war anyway?"

"War is one big bear trap. I don't remember a second of it. I would just as soon that we never talk about that," Fredek answered.

"He doesn't want to talk about it," Anne said to Billy—with extra volume, so he would be sure to hear her across the middle treehouse.

"I *heard* the man," Billy said quietly.

Next Steps

The gang remained comfortably in Fredek's kingdom for seven days. When Billy's ankle recovered, conversations turned to strategy.

"What's your plan to get to Harrisonburg," Fredek asked.

"I think it's a *wet* one," Anne said, referring to the North River, which she still wasn't sure how they would tackle.

"What's *your* plan, Chubby?" Billy said to Fredek.

"If it were me, I'd hike down Mount Sidney to the trail head and set up camp right there just inside the edge of the woods. I'd send a couple of you into town to restock some supplies, so every person has a decent pair of shoes," Fredek said.

"Why wouldn't you go into town, yourself?" Billy asked.

"Well, you asked what I would do. If it were my choice, I'd put my feet up and relax while you and Anne go fetch supplies," Fredek laughed. "We'd take a good night's sleep inside the woods to set us up for the two-day trek to Weyer's Cave."

"*Two days?*" Josey said.

"Two days," Fredek repeated. There's an orphanage just outside the cave. We can sneak in there for any supplies we might need. The cave should have enough water and shelter. We'll be fine there for a couple of days."

"I guess Chubby here knows his stuff, after all," Billy said, patting Fredek on the back. The gang agreed on the plan.

"You didn't mention the wet part," Anne said. "The boat?"

"It won't be too hard to find a boat on the river's edge. If not, we'll make one," Fredek said.

"You make boats, too?" Anne asked.

"I've made them in my mind," Fredek answered.

"How comforting," Anne said sarcastically. "Can your mind just put us in Harrisonburg already?"

Sensing Anne's nervousness, Billy chimed in. "It'll be fine, Anne. Don't worry. I've made lots of boats." *It's not exactly a lie if it helps a person, right?* Billy thought.

The North River Legend

The gang packed up and headed to the trail head according to plan. On the journey, Fredek said, "I overheard a few old timers say there's a minister and his wife who live along the North River. Behind their homestead is a vine some people say is powerful."

"What's so powerful about a vine?" Rascal said.

"They say the fruit is more beautiful than any man can grow," Fredek answered.

"Beautiful fruit? I'm not following," Billy said.

"Do you think we'll see it?" Rascal said, eager to believe the legend.

"I don't know," Fredek said. "I never have. But, it's more than just beautiful fruit. It grows on its own. The flavors are so brilliant they're barely recognizable. The old guys say this has been going on as long as they've lived here, and as long as their family had lived here before that. They say at night, the leaves glow."

Rascal remembered a scripture from the book of Revelation that he'd heard from the pulpit one Sunday:

And he shewed me a pure river of water of life, clear as crystal, proceeding out of the throne of God and of the Lamb. In the midst of the street of it, and on either side of the river, was there the tree of life, which bare twelve manner of fruits, and yielded her fruit every month: and the leaves of the tree were for the healing of the nations. And there shall be no more curse: but the throne of God and of the Lamb shall be in it; and his servants shall serve him: And they shall see his face; and his name shall be in their foreheads. And there shall be no night there; and they need no candle, neither light of the sun; for the Lord God giveth them light: and they shall reign for ever and ever.

Rascal thought about the scripture, then he thought about his own glowing knife. "They *glow?* The leaves ... they *glow?*" he asked.

"That's what they say, alright. They glow a bright green. And, a sparkling brook flows across the same land, but no one knows where the water originates. I mean, there's no well there or nothin'!" Fredek said.

The gang kept walking quietly, each lost in their own wonder on what Fredek had just said. The foolishness of Fredek's words rang loudly in his ears. *They must think I'm out of my mind,* he thought. "I mean, that's just what they *say.* It's not like I believe in special glowing vines or anything," he added with a chuckle, as a tiny drop of shame welled up in him. *Glowing vines,* he thought. *I suppose I'm crazy for believing it … but what if it's true?*

Rascal felt his spirits fall with Fredek's. He wanted to be rational, like Fredek, but secretly, he hoped the story was true. "Vines or not," Rascal said, "at least the minister might give us a place to regroup before our last train stop at Pleasant Valley."

The gang agreed.

"Billy," Josey said, "You're quiet over there. Is everything okay?" Lost in thought, Billy kept walking, like he hadn't heard a word. "Billy?" she asked again.

"Oh, me? Yeah. Me? I'm good," Billy said.

"Sure, you are," Josey said.

"I guess I was just realizing how close we are to actually making it," Billy said. "We're actually going to make it," he said.

"He's positively giddy!" Anne said, listening in.

Billy smiled and rolled his eyes. "We found lodging, water—"

"We held off the beasts!" Rascal added.

"Right! … and met this fella," Billy said, rubbing the top of Fredek's head. "It's almost like someone's looking out for us."

"I'd say that's God," Josey said. "And, it's about time we thank Him."

"What, you mean like pray?" Billy asked.

"Well?" Josey said.

"You know what? Josey … you're right." Billy stopped walking and laid down his sack on a nearby rock. "Hey, Rasc. Think you can break up a few of those old branches?" The gang gathered flat stones and assembled them to form a circular pit. Rascal filled the pit with sticks about the length of his arm. "Perfect, just like Bible times," Billy said.

"What is it?" Fredek asked.

"It's an altar!" Billy said, striking his flint against one of the stones to ignite a few dried leaves.

Fire began to grow in the center of the pit. "Anyone know a good Bible song?" Billy asked.

"I don't think you have to sing," Josey said.

Just then Anne, who had watched the whole gang assemble this strange monument, remembered one of the first songs Old Lady Kathryn taught her on the piano and began to sing, "Uhmaaaaazing grace, how sweeeet the sound that saved a wretch like me ..."

The others, having learned the song from innumerable Sundays in the pew, themselves, instantly remember the tune and joined in, "I once was lost but now am found, was blind, but now I see."

"Let us pray," Billy said, trying to recreate the scenes he'd seen so many times at the town church. "Lord, I reckon You are with us. I think You brought us to water and to shelter and to good people along our journey. So, we stopped here to ... uh ... well, ... we built You this ... *altar!*" Billy looked up to check the expressions of the people around him. They all stood with their heads bowed and eyes closed. "... to say *thank You!*" Billy added. "So, thank You." Billy looked up again, satisfied with his first public prayer. Seeing his friends still with heads bowed, he realized he'd forgotten one important part. "Oh, yeah, and AMEN!"

"Amen," the gang repeated, as they lifted their gaze.

"Like *that?*" Billy asked Josey. "I mean, do you think He liked that?"

"Yes, Billy," Josey said, smiling. "I think He did."

After the prayer, the gang hiked to a good stopping place for camp. They talked about all the good things that had happened on their journey—even how the bad things (like getting caught sneaking watermelons) somehow ended in good things, too.

They all knew the North River was coming up, but first, they'd have to reach Weyer's Cave.

Ask Yourself

1. Billy wasn't sure the gang wouldn't run into another pack of coyotes but decided not to worry about what he couldn't control. How does a focus on what you can do help control fear of the unknown?

2. Fredek said people call him "Chubby," but Josey, sensing he didn't like his nickname, chose not to use it. How do names people call you affect the way you think of yourself?

3. Chubby avoided talking about the war. What are a few healthy response options when people ask you about things that are too painful to talk about?

Outdoor Survival Tips: Plan for the Unexpected

To *improvise* means to use available resources to address an immediate problem. Be prepared to improvise as you pack for your journey by including multi-function gear, like a sharp pocket knife, iodine (for marking paths *and* disinfecting wounds), a small sturdy rope, heat-support supplies (like flint, a magnifying lens, waterproof matches), cloth (for wrapping, drying, staying warm) and a light source. Versatile supplies will help you handle unexpected circumstances on your journey.

Follow Billy's Journey

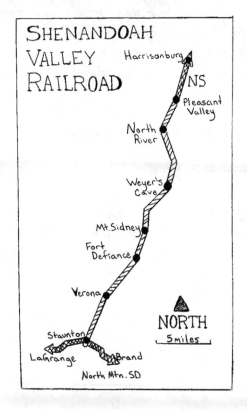

Chapter Seven

Weyer's Cave, VA

Lizzy Finds Her Voice

Dear Ma and Pa,

We're glad to be moving again. Not even wild coyotes could stop us.

Our new friend, Chubby, showed us three tree houses that he actually built by himself. They're built in cucumber trees and overlook Mount Sidney.

It's great to have a real builder on board. It seems like this gang was meant to keep growing, because after a couple weeks together, Chubby feels like part of the family. He knows his way around these parts, so he's leading us to Weyer's Cave. I bet they'll have bats—the girls will love that.

The gang and I reflected on the good things that have happened on our journey. Honestly, I thought it was a poor use of time, but at least it would be quick. But, two hours later, we were still coming up with things to be thankful for on this trip. By then, I didn't care about the time, I was actually enjoying myself. Know what else? It put me in a better mood than I've been in in a long time.

Even in the hard stuff, we knew someone was with us. Josey's pretty
sure that someone is God. Think so?
I love you,
Billy.

The Incredible Ms. Josey

"Only about a mile to go," Fredek said. "I'd say we've crossed about two miles of trail already."

"What's that?" Josey said, pointing to a collection of trees with leaves beginning to show autumn color.

"I don't see anything but trees," Billy said. The others agreed.

Shocked that the others didn't see what she saw supernaturally, Josey discreetly peeked at the thimble she was still wearing on a string around her neck. *I thought so,* Josey thought. The thimble's glow confirmed she was on to something. "Guys, trust me. We need to check this out. Follow me."

"I'm always up for an adventure, but aren't we a little close to nightfall to be sightseeing?" Billy said.

"C'mon, Billy," Fredek said. "We have time."

As the gang crossed past the edge of the tree line, Billy said, "Should we see something by now?"

"Look at *that!*" Fredek yelled. "Is it some kind of church?"

"It's a monastery," Josey said.

"Our Lady of the Angels Monastery," Fredek called, reading a large sign on the monastery grounds. "What's a *monastery?*"

"Wait!" Billy said. "There are *monks* in there?"

"Or *nuns,*" Josey said.

Meanwhile, Anne already had made her way up to the massive wooden door. Just as the group discussed a plan of action, she raised her fist to the door and gave it three good pounds.

"What are you doing, Anne?" Billy said in his loudest whisper.

"Well, we want to know who's in there, don't we?" Anne said.

Not glowing, Rascal thought, as he checked his knife for a cue on how to proceed. *I guess it's safe here.*

After several minutes, a woman came to the door. She pulled it back slightly—enough to see the flock of young travelers. "Ohhh, *children!*" she exclaimed and closed the door. The gang looked at each other in confusion.

"Well?" Billy said.

"Give her a minute," Anne said, too proud to admit that the greeting had surprised her, too.

Another few minutes passed, and the nun returned to the large wooden door. She slid open a small square the size of a bread roll and began to speak. The nun's warm countenance was so powerful that, even though they could only see her eyes and the bridge of her nose, they all felt a physical presence of love.

"Children, I'm Sister Maria," she said. "And, who are you?"

"We're out admiring the colors of autumn," Billy said, trying to answer before any of the others revealed their actual situation. "They *are* beautiful, aren't they?"

"And, however did you find us?" Sister Maria asked.

"Josey found you!" Rascal blurted out.

"And, you must be Josey," Sister Maria said. "Why don't you come with me a moment?"

"Now, I don't know about that," Billy said, feeling strangely protective. "We pretty well stick together."

"Of course," Sister Maria said, "I'll give you a moment to discuss."

At once, both Rascal and Josey said, "It's fine." They looked at each other—both a little surprised that the other one had the same good sense about the monastery.

"Fine? Really? Just send her off with strangers?" Billy responded, confounded.

"They're *nuns*, Billy," Anne said.

Billy froze, then looked at the faces of Rascal, then Anne, then back to Rascal again who held firm in his expression. "Well, if you say so," Billy said finally.

Josey and Sister Maria disappeared behind the large wooden door. "Just remember to come back," Billy called after Josey, "Sundown and all, *remember?*"

Rosie and Lizzy

As quickly as the door closed, two young girls walked right up to the gang and seated themselves on the gang's old suitcase.

"Hello?" Billy said, looking down at them. The girls grinned.

"I'm Lizzy. This is Rosie." Lizzy said. "Don't trouble yourself getting a word out of her. She's not a talker."

The two girls were darling little creatures. They endeared themselves to the gang, taking their seats on the gang's luggage and lingering the entire time Josey was away.

Josey Finds Favor

Meanwhile, inside the monastery, Josey and the nuns acquainted themselves. "So, how did you *really* find us?"

"Wye, Sister ...," Josey began, "It's as large as day. Who could miss it?"

"My dear, I, myself, would be hard-pressed to find this monastery again were I to step off of these grounds. It is one with the landscape, well camouflaged, and guests are highly infrequent for that reason," the nun responded.

Josey nodded but did not understand the nun's words—for her vision of the monastery was clear from nearly a mile off from the land. For the sake of agreeability, she agreed, "Yes, I reckon it was the sweet smell of burning wood chips that drew me this way." Josey still wondered what purpose the nun had in inviting her inside the grounds.

"The last shall be first," said Sister Maria.

"The last?" Josey asked.

"Those are the words of our Lord, Josey, 'The last shall be first' "Sister Maria repeated. She held her gentle gaze on Josey.

Not sure what to say, Josey continued walking for a bit, then said, "You mean *me*, Sister Maria?"

Josey's family had been the property of others as long as she'd been alive. Her clothes told the story of the many garments they comprised before Josey joined them together with thread.

"The Lord favors you, dear," the nun said.

Josey took hold of Sister Maria's hand. As they walked the corridors of the monastery, Josey felt a sense of something surround her—something beyond the love of the nuns. *Is this the Lord's favor?* she wondered. A message came to her mind—the one where the apostle Paul taught some of the first followers of Jesus that the way of Jesus brings life greater than the life one achieves through simply doing the right thing under the religious law. *Where the spirit of the Lord is, there is liberty*, she thought. Those were the words of Paul to the Corinthians. (II Corinthians 3:17). Suddenly, having been legally free for a number of years already, Josey felt truly free in body and spirit.

When Sister Maria and Josey arrived back to the entrance, Sister Maria said, "This is a house of the Lord, dear one. Do you think your friends are comfortable with that?"

"Oh, yes! Well, yes, *mostly*," Josey sputtered. "Well, almost all of us. Chubb—I mean, *Fredek*, is, wye … he's on the fence."

Sister Maria smiled with warm eyes and pressed her lips together, so as not to giggle. "Well, among other things, our Lord is a gentleman. Likewise, we offer these gifts to your friends without force. Please let your friends know you are all welcome to stay in our covering.

Josey clenched at her neck where the thimble glowed beneath her collar. "You do know you have authority to make the glow stop," said Sister Maria.

"The glow? No ... I ..." Josey stammered, concerned that Sister Maria had discovered the thimble Josey wished to keep secret.

Confused but rushed, Josey whispered, "Please stop. Please!" in the direction of her necklace.

"There's no need to panic. When you embrace your authority, you can activate it with calm, competent confidence. But, how is it you happened upon such a blessing as this thimble that glows?" asked Sister Maria.

"It's not mine, actually," Josey answered. "I'm holding it ... for a friend."

Sensing Josey's hesitation, Sister Maria said, "Well, I'm sure you will know when it's time for this blessing to make its way back home."

"Yes, Ma'am," Josey answered, relieved.

The Gang Enters the Monastery

Josey delivered the message of hospitality to the gang and ushered them into the monastery where the nuns showed each person to his or her own room for the evening. "What about those little runts?" Billy asked, referring to Rosie and Lizzy. But, Josey had no clue what he meant and urged him forward.

"I'm Sister Claire," one nun said to Anne. "I'll show you where your animals will be comfortable for the night." Sister Claire led Anne to a small barn behind the monastery. "There's plenty of bedding and food for the animals here, and everyone seems to get along nicely," she said, running her hand down the velvety snout of a large brown cow.

"Thank you!" Anne said, releasing the cats and dogs to choose their spots for the evening.

In the monastery, the children found their rooms to be pristinely clean and welcoming. The beds were comfortable, and the nuns kept a wealth of warm water and supplies for washing up.

"Join us for breakfast at 7:30am tomorrow, promptly after prayers," Sister Maria invited. "Now, be blessed as you rest," she said in a sort of speaking prayer.

The next morning, the gang awoke courtesy of a system of bells linked to a common cable. Chubby, Josey, Rascal, Anne and Billy heard prayers as they descended stairs to the dining space.

"Eggs! … *Bacon!*" Fredek called.

"Calm down, Chubby-boy!" Anne said.

At the breakfast table, the gang found soft-boiled eggs, crispy bacon, hand-churned butter and fluffy biscuits just emerging from the pot-belly stove equipped with a flat sheet of iron for cooking. The children enjoyed blueberry jam and fresh apple juice from the apples grown on the monastery grounds.

"What do you think, Rascal?" Billy said. "Is this as good as the food back at the dormitory?"

"No fooling!" Rascal said, wide-eyed and smiling. "I can't remember ever eating this well," he answered between bites, never looking up from his plate.

"Dear ones," Sister Maria interjected. "Let's discuss your plans. We must make sure you are cared for, so how do you plan on joining up with your guardians?"

Billy normally let Anne field the grown-up questions, but he answered nonetheless. "Ma'am … Sister … We're going up to Harrisonburg. Our … *family* is there."

"Your family?" Sister Maria said.

"Well, yes. We have a mix of kin in that area, and the rest of us will … Well, we'll share," Billy answered, proud of his ingenuity under pressure.

With a pleasant smile and affirmative nod, Sister Maria asked, "And, do you have the resources you will need for your journey?"

"Well, that's just it," Billy said. "You wouldn't have use of a few extra hands over the week, so as we could make a little money for the last leg of our journey, would you?"

Anne, who had held her tongue longer than she'd ever be capable of doing before that moment, spoke up. "Sister Maria, we are all on our own journey. Somehow, they match up to take us to Harrisonburg, and that's all we know until we arrive," she said. Anne continued for nearly thirty-five minutes covering in colorful detail all of the wild antics that resulted in each new member of the gang.

"Well, heaven's sake!" said Sister Claire, "Aren't they a troupe to behold."

"A blessed bunch they are," Sister Maria answered. "Children, an abundance of work keeps this monastery in proper order. For ten days, you're welcome to stay and work to that end. You'll each earn thirty cents per day and join us for three hot meals," Sister Maria smiled at Rascal and Chubby who were visibly delighted to hear her speak of meals. She continued, "... meals. with which you will assist," she added. "Boys, you'll also serve with Sister Claire and the others with the animals, the harvest and the dairy."

The boys nodded in unison.

After the first morning of work at the monastery, the gang cleaned up and took their seats at the dining table where the two small girls from the day before were already seated.

"Rosie, isn't it?" Billy said to the young girl.

Josey, unsure how the gang knew the young girls, extended her hand, "Rosie, I'm Josey."

"Glad to meet you, Josey," Lizzy said. "This here is Rosie, but she is content to be quiet most times. Ain'tcha, Rosie?" Lizzy prodded, displaying her maturity to the gang of older children.

"No need for rudeness, Lizzy," Anne said sternly.

Lizzy looked at Anne, "Rude? Wye, I'm just trying to get some manners out of the thing!" Lizzy replied.

Billy jumped between the two girls before they could escalate their exchange, knowing (from personal experience) how Anne tended to settle conflicts with a fist when it came to defending another person's honor. "Now, ladies, I think our hearts are in the right places, here. Let's try that again," Billy said.

"Rosie," Josey said to Rosie, extending her hand to the other ten-year old.

Rosie nodded with a slight smile.

From afar, Sister Maria approached the group. "Little ones, Jesus showed his love and service to his disciples by washing their feet in John

13. We do the same, like the verse says, 'If I then, your Lord and Teacher, have washed your feet, you also ought to wash one another's feet.' Now, won't you join us this evening for a ceremonial foot washing?" Sister Maria asked.

The group felt caught in the midst of their bickering. They looked around to see how the invitation struck the others. Without speaking a word, the group members understood they would all participate in the foot washing, because something about Sister Maria's invitation didn't feel optional at all. Lunch continued as normal, and they all reconvened after dinner for the event.

The Foot Washing

Twenty-one people in all attended the ceremonial foot-washing. Billy, Anne and Sister Maria presided.

"Here, Billy," Sister Maria said. "Please fill these bowls with warm water as I find this evening's passage."

Sister Maria turned to John chapter 13 and began to read the passage describing Jesus's example of foot washing in the Gospel. When she finished, she took her place, along with Anne and Billy, behind one of the three large wooden bowls and called the group to line up. In front of each bowl, stood seven people.

Anne didn't see Lizzy, so, without making a fuss, she washed the feet of the seven people in her line. "I'll see to it the bowls are emptied and cleaned," she said to Sister Maria.

"Thank you, child," Sister Maria said.

Anne carried her bowl carefully down a corridor, looking for Lizzy. "Lizzy," she said, seeing Lizzy crumpled up in a corner.

Lizzy didn't respond. She remained seated in the corner with her arms clutching her knees, which were pulled up to her chest as she shook her head *no*.

Having compassion on Lizzy's fear, Anne said, "It's okay, Lizzy. Jesus doesn't force anything on his children, and I won't force anything on you." Anne wished Lizzy understood how to receive good things the way children receive good gifts from their father, but she knew also that some skills can't be rushed.

Lizzy's face softened, and she looked up. "… but maybe you can help me clean the bowls?" Anne said.

A smile peeked out from Lizzy's stern face. Surprised that Anne (who had been so feisty with Rosie a few hours prior) was so easy to talk to, Lizzy stood and took a bowl from Anne.

"I'll come right back. Stay here," Anne instructed, as she returned to the sanctuary to collect another bowl. The girls walked together to the back of the monastery where they began to empty the water near the garden.

"So, did you and Rosie make peace at all?" Anne asked.

Lizzy nodded *yes*.

"Lizzy, may I wash your feet with this remaining water before we give back to the ground?" Anne asked.

Lizzy looked at Anne. Her big eyes filled with tears that didn't spill out onto her face, and she nodded again.

"We'll do it right here," Anne said. She took hold of the bowl from Lizzy and filled it from the cistern nearby. Then, she returned to Lizzy and knelt down. Using the towel, still tucked in her arm from the ceremony, Anne placed both of Lizzy's small feet into the bowl.

Lizzy's eyes were closed tightly, as Anne poured water over Lizzy's feet. Anne looked down to see that one of Lizzy's feet had a slight deformity—an extra toe. Anne's heart flooded with compassion and she continued the ceremony. She looked up at Lizzy's face and recited a verse that had been spoken in the evening's ceremony: "… he that is the greatest among you, let him be as the younger; and he that is chief, as he that doth serve." (Luke 22:26)

Just then, Lizzy peeked between her eyelids to see Anne drying her feet and smiling. Lizzy smiled slightly, as if to say *thank you*.

Lizzy felt like she could trust Anne, and Anne felt the same toward Lizzy. That private exchange brought them together more like sisters than new friends. From the sanctuary, they heard a woman's voice—one which they hadn't heard before.

"Let's go back!" Anne said. And, the girls hurried back to the others.

"To those of you who do not know me, my name is Sister Louada. For 365 days, I have embraced silence as a vow that I might more earnestly focus on the Lord. Lest you think me noble, I am rather a quiet person by nature, so the personal cost for my year of silence was small," she added. The room giggled. Tonight, I would like to share a message:"

The spirit animates the body, Webster's dictionary says. It relates to ecclesiastical things (of the church) rather than temporal things (of the world). How easily one can seek spirituality in and of itself and miss the greater goodness of God.

In Isaiah 61, verse 1, the Scripture says, "The Spirit of the Lord GOD is upon me; because the LORD hath anointed me to preach good tidings unto the meek; he hath sent me to bind up the brokenhearted, to proclaim liberty to the captives, and the opening of the prison to them that are bound."

And, in Isaiah 64, verse 4, we read, "For since the beginning of the world men have not heard, nor perceived by the ear, neither hath the eye seen, O God, beside thee, what he hath prepared for him that waiteth for him."

Know, young ones, we are encouraged to seek a nameless, faceless spiritual center within oneself, that is not the God of the Bible—the Messiah, Jesus Christ. Faith, rooted in the Gospel of Jesus is more powerful than simple positive thinking. And the hope of glory is more than a vain wish. As followers of Christ, we seek not simply to attain a happy life, we bring God's Kingdom to bear on this earth until Jesus returns to set creation right for eternity.

This sounds like foolishness to some. In fact, I Corinthians 1, verse 18, says, "For the preaching of the cross is to them that perish foolishness; but unto us which are saved it is the power of God." And, in chapter 2, verse 14, Paul continues, "The person without the Spirit does not accept the things that come from the Spirit of God but considers them foolishness, and cannot understand them because they are discerned only through the Spirit.

Dear ones, do not be lulled into mere spirituality—spiritual things without the power to save. All these things mean nothing outside of Jesus the Christ.

(John) Calvin said, "The human mind is a perpetual factory of idols." But, what are idols if they are not golden calves?

Idols are where we place our trust outside of God. Matthew chapter 6, verse 21, says, "For where your treasure is, there your heart will be also."

We can't help but attach our hearts to the thing we trust to save us. But, that is dangerous, dear ones. There is no person and no thing perfectly trustworthy outside of the Lord, God, who loves perfectly without fail.

Every person—even an atheist—will trust something for salvation. Maybe it's a philosophy or a hefty inheritance. Maybe it's a lifetime of good works towards one's fellow man. Those efforts have no power to save. They are nothing more than idolatrous pursuits. When we seek God within ourselves, we can't help but create idols.

Let us remember, Dear Ones, to put our faith in the Lord God of the Universe who has given us His only son, Jesus Christ, so that we can receive perfect love and carry it forth to a hurting world.

The room was silent. Chubby looked at the others. *Are they really buying into all of this?* He wondered. Then, the sweet sound of footsteps filled the sanctuary, as two nuns stepped forward to hug Sister Louada. After her lengthy address, Sister Louada remained silent for the rest of the week.

Ten days came and went rather quickly for the gang. Altogether, they had earned 15 dollars between daily earnings and odd jobs. The boys gladly filled their haversacks with dried meats and fruits, hard tack and freshly waxed cheeses, while the gang said their tearful goodbyes following the best breakfast they had eaten to date. "Thank you for your hospitality," Billy said on the last morning, leading the gang in gracious farewells, truly grateful for the clothing and generous portions of food the nuns had shared.

"Every good thing we have to give, is a gift the Lord has given to us," Sister Maria said.

"You mean, *God* gave you gifts for … *us?*" Fredek asked?

"Dear Fredek," Sister Maria said, looking up at the large boy sweetly, "The Lord knows your need."

Fredek looked at Sister Maria's eyes as she spoke. He'd heard lots of untruths during his lifetime, but something about the way she spoke directly to him caused him to believe she might be telling the truth.

Tagalongs

The gang stepped out of the monastery gates with their eyes set on what was before them. Anne hung back a few steps, seeing Rosie and Lizzy peeking out from behind a nearby tree.

"Come with us!" Anne summoned. The girls looked at each other then back at Anne.

"Don't you go getting soft, Rosie," Lizzy said to Rosie, quietly. "We have everything we need right here."

"Everyone needs a family," Anne added, not having heard what Lizzy whispered. "And this is about as close to family as any of us have right now. *Follow us!"*

Rosie looked down, heavy with hopes freshly dashed for the day Lizzy will let them connect with others, and ran away deep into the woods. A few seconds later, Lizzy followed, and the tree that once partially hid the two girls was left with nothing to hide.

Not able to wait any longer without losing sight of her gang, Anne marched away from the monastery. She whispered a short prayer.

Deep in the woods, Lizzy caught up with Rosie. "Thatta girl," Lizzy said, commending Rosie for running away from Anne's invitation. "We're just fine on our—"

"WE'RE NOT FINE!" Rosie shouted.

Lizzy stopped speaking, shocked at Rosie's outburst.

Rosie began to sob, loudly. "We're *not* fine," she repeated, this time in a whimper. "We should have gone."

The Last Leg

"Whatcha thinkin' about, Chubby?" Billy called from a few yards behind Fredek as they trekked toward Weyer's Cave.

Fredek couldn't help but reflect on Sister Louada's words—she only had one batch of them, after all. And, they seemed to go on forever. But, somehow, all those words kept even Fredek's drifting attention. *I could just tell him that I can't get those words out of my head,* Fredek thought.

"Oh, nothin'," Fredek said, ignoring his own thoughts. Summoning the gang to plow ahead with one wave of his long muscled arm, he shouted, "We're getting close to the cave—only about a mile to go now!"

When the gang reached the entrance, Rascal and Anne decided to enter first to locate a flat location for sleeping. Rascal had learned by this time to consider his knife for these sorts of decisions. Its glow had saved them so many times before. As they explored the twisting arteries of the cave, Rascal paid close attention to the blade. It never glowed.

"It's safe here," Rascal said.

"What's that? Did you find a good sleeping spot?" Anne said, "because I think I found a good one over here, too."

Rascal had almost forgotten to look for flat spots—preoccupied by his scan for danger. "Wye, that looks near perfect to me. Let's head back and tell the gang," he said.

Only six minutes of exploration confirmed to the two explorers the safety of their new shelter. After finding a few suitable landings to set up for the night, the two backtracked to the mouth of the cave to retrieve the rest of the group.

"How does it look?" Billy called ahead to the returning explorers.

"This will suit us, alright. There's flat space for bedding about thirty yards in," Rascal said. "Ten yards deeper, we got water!"

"*Water?!*" Anne said.

"That's great!" Billy said. "Did you test it?"

"Looks like sweet, clean water to me," Rascal said. "We'll have a place to drink and clean up. What's more is the pool is surrounded by a good ten feet of sandy ground with a hole above—straight to the sky, so—"

"SO, we could build a fire right there beside the pool!" Billy interrupted

"YES!" Rascal said, proud of their find.

"Well, we had better gather up some wood, then. Let's get to work!" Anne said.

Billy and Josey gathered wood and delivered it about forty yards into the cave to the edge of the pool. The last remnant of daylight visible from inside the cave faded quickly as the two worked to light the fire.

The gang gathered around the fire talking, eating and enjoying their new environment with appropriate trepidation.

"What was *THAT?!*" Josey said, "Did you hear that? It was a rustling, coming from the mouth of the cave."

Rascal checked his knife. It wasn't glowing

"C'mon, Rascal," Billy said "Let's take a look," he said, as he extracted two burning sticks from the fire to serve as torches.

As they turned to trek to the mouth of the cave, two figures emerged from the darkness. "STOP THERE!" Billy shouted. Rascal, confident of his safety, walked ahead toward the figures without speaking. With every step, his torch shed more light on the frozen subjects, until gradually, the details of their faces clarified.

"Rosie?" Rascal said in disbelief. "It's Rosie!" he called back to Billy. "Rosie and Lizzy!"

"Is that a fact," Billy said, relieved, amused and maybe a small bit annoyed. "Well, c'mon girls. I suppose you have a story to tell." He turned around and headed back, mumbling to himself, "and I have a fire to tend."

All four made their way to the fire. Anne and Josey had seen the exchange but couldn't understand what had been said. As soon as she recognized Lizzy's face and small stature, she jumped up and ran to her.

"Lizzy! How did you get here? Rosie!" Anne said, as she hugged both girls.

"Please don't be upset with us. You were right," Lizzy said. Everyone froze and looked at Rosie who had not spoken a single word prior to this point. "We don't have any family on earth, but if you're still willing to be our family, we *accept!*" she said.

The gang gathered around the two girls, and Anne looked at Lizzy who had been so adamantly against journeying with the gang.

Lizzy spoke up. "As you can see," Lizzy said smiling, "Rosie found her own thoughts. And, truth be told, I am grateful she did. We might have stayed alone in those trees forever if she hadn't."

"Well?" Anne began. "Do we need to vote?"

"No vote," Billy said. "Looks like we're a gang of *seven!*"

The group enjoyed another hour by the fire with food and stories until fatigue caught up with them and they decided to settle into their separate sleeping areas. Fredek, who hadn't spoken for a while said, "Wait? Aren't we going to say *thank you?*"

"*Thank you?*" Billy said.

"Well, if God gives us all good things," Fredek began, "… and a couple of new travelers are good—"

"*Yeah?*" Billy said.

"—and they found us safely and all. And maybe we're a good thing to them, too," Fredek theorized.

"*Yeah?*" Billy said.

"Well, I just think a *thank you* is in order," Fredek said.

"To … *God?*" Billy asked.

"To God," Fredek said.

Billy, surprised to hear Fredek acknowledge the good provisions of God, looked at Anne who smiled back at him and gestured at him to respond. "Well, YES. Of COURSE!" Billy said. "Let's pray!"

The gang gathered and bowed their heads. One by one, each person thanked God for every good thing of the day. Fredek looked at his feet illuminated by the glow of the shrinking fire as he listed nearly a hundred blessings of the day. After seventy or eighty items, the other members started to lift their heads and look up at each other. A minute later, Fredek wrapped it up, "—in the name of Jesus Christ our Savior, we pray. Thanks, again! Sincerely, Fredek!"

"Goodnight, everyone!" Fredek bid with a smile and a wave. He paused, "What?" he asked, realizing the others were still staring at him.

"Well, … Chubby … that was quite a list," Billy said.

"Quite a *long* list," Lizzy added.

"Ohhh," Fredek laughed. "Was it? Maybe I should have warned you. I had a lot of *thank you's* to make up for." Fredek laughed as he took his supplies to his sleeping spot—five yards closer to the mouth of the cave to allow him to keep watch for any intruders or animals that might already be living in the cave.

The gang laughed as the flutter of bat wings seemed to clap for Fredek as he made his bed. The North River was less than a mile away from the cave. For the next two days, the gang planned their river journey. They estimated they would need a boat big enough to hold the seven passengers, the three small animals and one hundred pounds of supplies.

On day three, the gang woke up, ready to ride the river to Harrisonburg, and all at once, they heard a beautiful voice. It sounded like an angel. Without speaking, the gang gestured to each other to inch closer to the sound until they discovered the source. It was Lizzy.

Amazing grace! how sweet the sound,
That saved a wretch; like me!
I once was lost, but now am found,
Was blind, but now I see.

'Twas grace that taught my heart to fear,
And grace my fears relieved;
How precious did that grace appear
The hour I first believed!

The sweet song echoes throughout the twists and turns of the cave—off of every surface, so that the echoes seemed to be the songs of the very rocks that surrounded them.

"Did you know she could sing like that?" Fredek asked Rosie.

"Me? I don't even think *she* knew that gift was inside of her," Rosie said, eyes fixed on Lizzy.

Ask Yourself

1. Sister Maria exercised wisdom getting to know Josey before she invited the entire gang to enter the monastery. Why is it important to get to know people before you decide if they are trustworthy? How do you know you can trust God?

2. Jesus told His disciples in Matthew chapter 20 that, "the last shall be first." How does this truth apply to Fredek's delay in recognizing the Lord's blessing in his life?

3. Think back to the foot-washing ceremony. Lizzy had a hard time receiving that gift. Why is it hard to allow others to serve us?

4. Why did Lizzy go so long without using her voice? What gifts might God have put inside of you?

Outdoor Survival tips: Fire Safety

Fire provides heat and light, but danger exists without careful preparation of a fire pit. Use rocks, sand or dirt to contain the fire. Make sure there is plenty of ventilation but not too much powerful wind. Build fires away from flammable brush or dry trees. Finally, gather enough dry wood to last all night, then add three more pieces—just to be safe!

Follow Billy's Journey

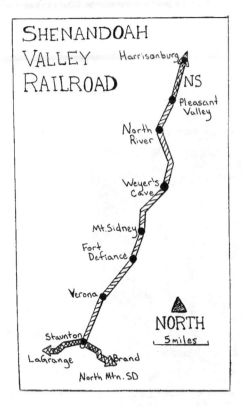

Chapter Eight

North River, Virginia

Reverend Timothy and the Inexplicable Vine

Dear Ma and Pa,

Our gang now consists of Rascal, Anne, Chubby, Josey, and, now, Lizzy with the voice of an angel—plus Rosie, who was a little rough around the edges when we first met her. But, you know I'm no saint, either.

We're about to journey from our cave home toward the North River. I hope our food lasts until we reach our first river stop—only about three days' worth left before we'll need to rely on our fishing abilities. Fish sure gets old quick, though.

Rosie came up with the idea for our raft. I'm full of excitement for our river journey. The water is still fairly warm, but the air is cooler than normal for this time of year, which could mean trouble for us. The locals tell me that sometimes when cool air hits a warm front, a wicked tornado forms.

I hate to admit it, but I need help. The gang will need a sturdy raft—one that can handle the river, yes, but also one that will hold all seven of us plus three animals! Just between you and me, I was hoping the solution would have come to me by now. I sure wish you were here. Please put in a good word that we make it to Pleasant Valley without any problems.

Love from Billy

Who Knows the Plan?

At the entrance of Weyer's Cave, Billy sat. Alone. The weight of the world pulled his shoulders down as he considered his team—the health of everyone; the kind of bait they might need to catch food on the river; Chubby's feelings about God; and, most of all, *the raft!* Meanwhile, the girls packed up for the day's hike to the river.

"Say, *Rascal! Chubby!*" Billy called out. "Come on over here for a minute. And, bring some wood with you, why don't you." The boys came near with a few handfuls of twigs. "I guess that's a start," Billy mumbled to himself. "Listen, fellas," he began. "I don't see any reason in burdening the girls with this, but we need a boat."

"Of *course*, we need a boat," Chubby said cheerfully.

"Right," Billy said. He took a long pause, considering how hard it would be to reveal that he didn't have a plan for making the boat they would need for their journey. He remembered a part of the Bible where Jesus told His disciples not to worry about what they would say when they were on trial, because God's Spirit would give them the words. *I sure hope God's Spirit has a few words for me today,* Billy wished in his heart. He opened his mouth to speak. "So, boys—"

"That's a GREAT idea!" Rosie exclaimed.

"Rosie! Where'd you—I didn't know you were *there!*" Billy said, concerned she would tell the others that he didn't have a plan and cause the girls to worry.

"The WAGON!" Rosie continued, "Didn't you say *wagon?* That's a great idea."

Billy nodded in agreement to buy a little time while Rosie spoke, wondering to himself, *Did I say* wagon? *What is she going on about?*

Rosie continued to explain the plan to the last detail. She described just where they could retrieve the wagon and horse they'd stored at the old farm, which wasn't too far away, and use it to easily transport their items to the bank of the North River, then disassemble the wagon and use the boards to build a sturdy raft. She described precisely the dimensions and supplies they would use to accomplish this. By the time Rosie finished speaking, the whole gang had gathered around.

Billy finally spoke. "Rosie," he began, "Now, *that's* a plan!"

"I'd say," Anne said. Then, looking at Josey, Anne murmured, "I was beginning to wonder if Billy had a plan for travelling that ol' river at all."

When the crowd scattered, Billy caught up with Rosie. "Hey, Rosie," he said. "You know that wasn't my idea, don't you?"

"What do you mean?" she said.

"I never said anything about a farmer in these parts or any wagon," he said.

"You didn't?" she said.

"Not once. How do you suppose you caught that idea anyhow? … *And how do you know about the ol' farmer?*" he asked.

"Well, the plan came to me so clearly, I thought I must have heard you boys say it," Rosie said. "This morning, I got away in the trees to pray before the sun came up, like I have seen the nuns do so often. I sang a little song to God and thanked Him for bringing friends to us. I felt the worries that filled my brain with chatter just fall out of my head, I suppose, and I was full of—"

"Full of *what?*" Billy asked.

"—just full of the sense that everything was good—things between God and me, things between the gang and me ... *everything!*" she said.

"I think they call that peace," Billy said.

"Peace! It *was* peace," Rosie said with a smile. "Then when I got back to the cave and heard you talking to Rascal and Chubby, I heard every detail of the boat we needed to build and how we needed to build it. I figured I had overheard you, but I guess—"

"God gave us the plan just in time," Billy said, patting Rosie on the back.

Another Night in the Cave

While Rascal and Fredek doubled back to the homestead to retrieve the horse and wagon from the bottom of Mount Sidney, Billy set up a fire for the gang's last night at the cave. He warmed a few scraps of dried beef from the day before—enough to fill the girls' stomachs for the night. When they'd had all they wanted to eat, the girls prepared their beds close to the fire.

"You'll keep watch?" Anne asked Billy.

"Yessiree," Billy said with an affirmative nod of the head.

A few hours later, Billy, realizing he'd nodded off, sat up quickly and stepped toward the mouth of the cave. "WHO'S THERE?" he called.

"It's us, y'old buzzard!" Fredek answered.

"What'd you do, *fly?*" Billy exclaimed. "I didn't expect you until tomorrow afternoon."

"It was clockwork," Rascal said, grabbing a few small tree limbs to build fencing for the horse. "Let's get this horse set up for the night and get some sleep."

The boys stacked branches in a large rectangle formation around the horse—leaving plenty of room for the horse to graze and rest before the next day's journey.

When morning came, Billy woke up, packed up his bedding and went to check on the horse. Surprised to find that Fredek had already awoken and begun packing, he thought, *what's he doin' sneaking around out here?*

"Well, look who is up and at 'em," Billy said finally.

"Oh, hiya, Billy. I thought I'd get us started.

"Either that, or you're fixin' to rob us!" Billy said somewhat jokingly.

Fredek stopped loading for a moment, offended at the suggestion, and looked at Billy. He found enough signs of sarcasm in Billy's expression to think nothing more of the comment, but inside Fredek wondered if Billy had read his mind.

"How about you pack up the food supplies. I have a spot for them right here in the corner," Fredek directed. Billy nodded as his joking thought returned more seriously, *surely that boy wouldn't rob us, would he?*

Billy returned to the cave to find everyone awake and packing up. They went out one by one to load their supplies into the wagon.

"I'll pack the blankets," Josey said. The gang thanked her and brought their bedding for her to fold and fit into the wagon. Her bulky load gave her plenty of cover to sneak the thimble case onto the wagon.

"Well, that didn't take long," Fredek said, gazing at the wagon packed high.

"I'll go stomp the fire," Billy said. He headed toward the cave and stopped when he heard a sound in the woods.

"Hey, Josey," Billy said quietly. He gestured for her to come take a look. "See anything?"

Josey peered through the woods. She had an extraordinary ability to see what others couldn't, but this was the first time someone had asked her to do it. She peered into the woods for several minutes before she saw anything. *Maybe I should make something up?* She wondered. *He must regret even asking me to help him—*

"Oh, there's a BOY!" Josey yelled, excited to have discovered something.

"Sshhh!" Billy said. "He won't *see* you, but he might hear you. Now, you say there's a boy out there?"

"Yes," Josey said. "He's short—legs like a horse—but hunched over. Looks like he's bent over a basin … a water basin, working. He's young, maybe 12, freckled all over, and dirty, very dirty. I see blonde shaggy hair and brown eyes—"

"You can see all that?" Billy said.

"—and a scar … on his *chin!*" Josey continued.

"A scar?!" Billy exclaimed. "You can see a scar? Now you're just making fun of me." Billy's volume increased as he spoke. Josey tried to hush him to no avail.

"Billy! He sees us." Josey said.

"Impossible," Billy said.

"Billy," Josey said with fear. "He's looking right into my eyes across all of this distance, I know he is. What should I do?"

Josey took her eyes off of the boy for a second to see what Billy wanted to do next.

"Hello," the boy said, suddenly standing one arm's length away.

"WHOA!" Billy said, jumping back. Josey tucked herself behind Billy. "Whoa, now, buddy," Billy continued, composing himself. "You gave us a bit of a scare." Billy's mind raced with wonder. *How did this boy cross such a distance in a single moment? He must not have been far after all.*

"My name is Gabe," the boy said, extending his hand, still dripping with water from the basin he'd been using when Josey saw him. He was strong and burly with short legs. He had brown eyes, and like Josey, he had eyesight like an owl. His hair was blonde and so shaggy it almost covered his freckles.

"Gabe, eh?" Billy fumbled, still trying to get his wits about him. "Nice to make your acquaintance," Billy said, shaking Gabe's hand. "And this is Josey," Billy said.

Gabe showed the two around the forest through the many trees and plants. Somehow, he knew every single stream—though he'd never seen them. "Wow, it's beautiful," Gabe said.

"You mean to say you've never been out this far?" Billy asked Gabe in disbelief.

"Oh, I ventured out once, and I ran smack into a spruce tree," Gabe said, gesturing to the scar on his chin. "Now, I stay near my master," Gabe said, "only going out as far as I need to find fresh water to clean my master's clothes. Looking down, Gabe saw that the gang's cat, Rhea, had approached. He lowered his hand to pet her, but she lunged at his hand with her one paw and an open mouth. "The clothes!" Gabe shouted, as the freshly laundered clothes fell to the muddy ground.

The group paused in silence to see what Gabe would do. After a few seconds, Gabe looked at Billy, "So, you said you wanted to see the forest? It looks like I'm in the market to find a new stream, myself."

Billy smiled.

"Follow me!" Gabe said, taking off at a swift pace.

"Oh, one sec. We'll follow you in the wagon," Billy said. "Josey, go have the girls climb into the wagon. Oh, and see which man wants to ride the horse first," he added.

"Which *man?*" Josey said, already heading toward the gang, smiling at Billy's choice of words.

"*What?* I'm taking care of this gang, ain't I? That's what a *man* does." Billy muttered with Josey too far off to hear. Billy was starting to think of himself as a man, but he wondered when the world would see him that way. Shouting forward to Gabe, Billy said, "It won't take two shakes to get everyone in the wagon." Gabe paused to wait for the gang to collect themselves.

A few minutes later, the gang approached with Fredek aboard the horse, girls in the wagon and Rascal following the travelers. Billy greeted them, "Gang, this is Gabe. He knows this forest, so he'll lead us into—"

"Wait!" Fredek yelled, "He's leaving without us!"

Billy stopped talking and let the wagon pass to catch up with Gabe. Then, he hung back with Rascal to keep watch from behind the wagon. Gabe led the gang to a clear creek packed with dozens of people swimming like lazy sunfish. Gabe turned back to the gang, "Let's go a bit further to find a private location to build your raft. There's a stream that connects just up ahead."

"This looks good," Billy called to Gabe as they arrived at a secluded area by a stream. "We'll build here," he said.

"Billy, I don't know about this. I'm not sure it's safe," Rascal said, seeing his knife glow.

"Is there danger here, Rascal?" Billy asked.

"I don't know. I mean, I don't know *for sure*. I *think* so," he said.

"Rascal, it sounds like your gut feeling is a little tongue tied. When you figure out what you think, let us know. In the meantime, we have to get this raft built, and this looks like as good of a place as any," Billy said, not seeing a reason to pass up such a perfect location.

"STAY IN THE WAGON!" Fredek called to the girls up ahead. The boys looked toward the wagon to see a large mangy wolf chasing Gabe into the stream. It looked to be about four feet from neck to tail, grayish brown with snarling teeth. Before Billy could say a word, Rascal took off running toward the wolf.

"RASCAL!" Billy called after him. "NO, RASCAL!" Billy wondered if Rascal was trying to prove his courage because of the comment he'd just made. *What have I done,* Billy thought. "COME BACK, RASCAL!" he shouted again.

Rascal disappeared out of view. Billy made it up to the wagon and told the girls everything would be fine—though he was not confident they would be. Then, they heard a blood-curdling scream.

Anne screeched. "Was that *him?!*"

Billy didn't answer. He couldn't believe what was happening. Just seconds before everything was perfect: the gang battled all of the challenges to start this last leg of the journey; they found best friends and generous help along the way; Gabe brought a mysterious comfort in these wily woods, but now ... *Is this really happening?* Billy thought. He stayed calm for the girls' sake, but he let them see the concern on his face. He felt they deserved that kind of honesty.

Billy remembered one time when his pa took him to play in the river and a copperhead nestled up around Billy's young legs. "Billy," Billy's Pa said. "Billy," he repeated, until Billy silently looked up into his father's big strong eyes. "Billy. Son. I love you. I'm going to give you directions, and you will follow them exactly. Then, we'll go home and have piping hot dinner with mother. Are you listening?" He then told him exactly how to safely get away from the copperhead without being bit by its poisonous bite.

Billy tried to be as gentle and reassuring to the girls as his Pa had been to him, giving him steady, clear instructions to lead him out of harm's way. *I wish you were here, Pa,* he thought.

Suddenly, Billy remembered what Rascal had tried to tell him, and his heart sunk. *Rascal knew we were in danger,* he thought.

Over the edge of a fallen tree, a figure emerged.

"GABE!" Josey called, full of hope that Rascal would follow. The gang waited in frozen silence. Just then, a second figure emerged.

Billy bolted from his position by the wagon to greet Rascal, running so swiftly he almost flew. He tackled Rascal with the force of a locomotive. "You were right, Rascal. You knew it all along. I should have listened. I'm sorry. I'll always listen to you. I'm sorry, Rascal," Billy rattled, ecstatic to see Rascal in one piece. "What's that, BLOOD? Rascal, are you okay?"

Rascal spoke for the first time after running to face the wolf. "It's blood." Rascal raised his powerful knife. Blood covered one edge of it and the handle.

"You really saved us, Rascal," Billy said. "And, I was lecturing *you* about guts. You're a regular wolf slayer!"

Billy hugged Rascal one more time with a strong pat on the back. Then, they walked to the wagon to tell the rest of the gang. From that day forward, that section of the North River was called "Wolf Slayers Bend."

The gang surrounded Rascal as he approached. Gabe warned them that wolves travel in packs and to be careful in that area. The gang decided to stay put to assemble their raft, and Gabe decided to warn the village of the wolf pack.

"Will your master be angry that you ventured so far away?" Josey asked.

"Yes, I suppose he may be," Gabe answered, "but I can't let the whole town be caught off guard. I will have to risk it."

The Village, the Raft and the Master

Gabe made his way to the village mayor to relay the story of the wolf.

"Son, you've done a good thing to warn us," the mayor said. "I'll assemble able bodied men to go take care of those prowling wolves before they make their way to our children."

Meanwhile, the gang set up camp by the stream. Rascal and Anne caught a few river trout and crayfish, while the rest of the gang built up a fire. Josey pulled out a few wild berries and peaches they'd been given at the monastery.

They had a filling meal and wondered if Gabe had faced any punishment for revealing his whereabouts. That night, they disassembled the wagon into sections that would become the raft.

The next morning, Gabe returned to the gang to find them drying clean clothes over the remains of the night's fire and assembling the raft. "I'm happy to see you, Gabe!" Billy said, smiling. "How did the village respond?" he asked. "I'm heading there, myself, as a matter of fact. How about you walk with me to see this horse?"

Gabe nodded. "For a handful of berries, I'll journey with you," he said with a smile. Billy grabbed berries and a few hunks of last night's fish, and then headed toward the village. Billy sold the horse to a local farmer for $20 and used the money for the last round of supplies. Billy and Gabe talked as they walked back to camp. Gabe described the calm intensity Rascal had as he slayed the wolf. Without warning, Gabe disappeared.

"Gabe?" Billy said, turning his head to look. On a nearby oak tree, Billy saw a note. Chuckling to himself, he ripped the note down to read it.

Gang,

You'll never know what your hospitality and friendship meant to me these last two days. I want you to know my Master was not angry with me for guiding you and walking with you in danger. In fact, He has created me for this purpose.

He, too, is with you always and loves you unconditionally—with an unfailing love unlike any other in creation. He will guide you in the ways of Truth by His Spirit. My Master has angels throughout the universe ready to deploy on behalf of the fatherless to keep you in perfect peace. So, that orange-eyed creature that sought to harm you early in your journey—we've bound him where he cannot harm you. No need to worry.

Yours by His command,

Gabe

P.S. Billy, you witnessed the power of Rascal's intuition. My master wants to reveal your power to you and show you how to use it for others' protection. When you are ready, just ask Him.

Billy shared the letter with the group—keeping the part about his power to himself. Then, they positioned the raft's rudder and tested the raft's makeshift "storage bin" to make sure it floats.

"Perfect!" Billy said. "It floats!" They tied up the raft for the night, crafted a few lean-to shelters for sleeping and supply storage and ate a good meal. "What an incredible day!" Billy said, reclining against a rock, full to the neck with fish and berries.

He wondered to himself about the part of the letter he hadn't shared with everyone. *What does Gabe mean "for others' protection"? Does that mean there's danger on the river?*

On the River

The next morning, Billy woke up early. He cleaned up camp and saw Rascal sleeping with the oars in his arms. *He must have fallen asleep while making a few finishing touches with his trusty knife,* Billy thought.

When everyone awoke, they loaded up their meager supplies onto the raft and pushed off from shore. "Am I the only one crossing my fingers?" little Lizzy said. The whole gang laughed.

The raft meandered gracefully down the river as the scenery changed. The trees were straight and pristine. The river's edge had patches of bright glowing green moss and active schools of fish darting in and out of the shadows. At times, the trees enveloped both sides of the river, seeming almost animated.

A little further down, another mangy wolf appeared—but this one was calm, restfully watching fish jump in the water. His purple mouth was fresh from the blueberry patch. The gang held their breath, because from their vantage point, they could see a family of baby bunnies getting close to the wolf.

"Oh, no, little bunnies!" Lizzy squeaked quietly, not wanting to disturb the wolf. "Will he eat them?"

The bunnies continued on their merry way until they bumped right into the wolf. They cuddled against his side and rolled over on their backs. One of them climbed atop the wolf's back, as if to get a better view of the raft as it passed by.

The gang was stunned. Anne said, "How on God's green earth could a vicious wolf be so kind to his dinner?"

"I wish I were fearless like those bunnies," Rosie said.

As the gang continued down the river, flowers opened into a rainbow of colors and textures. All day, the gang floated until they reached a fork in the river. On the left was a waterfall, and the river took a hard right. The gang stayed to the right, and when the river straightened back out, it opened into a large pool of water then narrowed again back into a stream.

On the right bank, a rock ledge protruded like a stage. On it were nine river otters organized in a clean row. They held rather grumpy faces—all except for one, which sat up and seemed to wave.

"Is that otter looking at us?" Rascal asked.

"Whatever he's looking at, he doesn't look all that bright to me," Billy answered.

Just then, the waving otter called, "Who goes there?"

Billy looked straight up at the otter in disbelief, "Uh ... I'm Billy Washita." Then he looked at the gang. "Are you fellas seeing this too, or have I lost my mind?" He turned back to the otter, "And what's your name, little creature?"

"Wye, I am the leader of the otters on this river, and you, Billy Washita, are trespassing."

Billy turned to the others. "You know, these obstinate otters clearly missed out on whatever it was that caused a wolf to befriend little rabbits a good ways back," Billy said.

Reverend Tim and Mama Carol

Just then, a man stepped out from the edge of the river. He was stately, with clean clothes and a face pristinely groomed. "What say you, young chicken hawks?"

Billy, not stirred at all, answered promptly. "My name is Billy Washita, and this here is my gang!" he said proudly, figuring that whether the man intended good or harm, he'd probably respond best to confidence.

"Well, welcome, little chicken hawks. We've been expecting you. I'm reverend Timothy, and you may call me Tim," he said, as he extended a hand by habit then quickly retracted, realizing the gang was too far down the river to return the handshake. "Come. Please tie up the raft here and come inside," he said.

"Now, just wait one minute," Anne said, slightly perturbed. "How did you know we were coming?"

"Young lady," Tim began, "the young lad Gabe visited our home and told us to expect you today."

That made sense to Anne and filled her with gratitude for God's watchful eye on the gang. She didn't know whether Tim knew Gabe was an angel, but she chose not to mention it—just in case.

The gang tied up the raft and began to unload a few basics. "Rex and Virginia have been itching to jump into this water all day, I think," Rascal said, looking at the gang's two dogs.

"Alright, you little fur balls. You, too! Go on!" said Billy, shooing the animals off the raft. The animals looked up at Billy.

"In good time," Rhea said, drawing out her words like a queen. The cat then looked at Rex the dog and said, "After you, your majesty!"

In amazement, Anne stared at Rhea.

"Have you never seen a talking cat?" Rhea said, leaping over the water to the river's edge.

Reverend Timothy invited the children in. "Please come meet my wife," he said. "The locals call her Mama Carol."

As the gang approached the entrance, the smell of peach cobbler filled their nostrils. "I smell cinnamon!" Fredek exclaimed. "And vanilla!" he added.

Inside, sat a table 15 feet long by five feet wide. On it were beautiful oak bowls and utensils with goblets full of clean water. A large salad of green and purple leaves graced the center of the table. Garden vegetables of all sorts adorned it.

"Smells like lamb stew," Fredek said quietly to Billy. Fredek pointed to an old cobblestone fireplace hosting a large black pot. The boys stepped discretely toward the pot and peered in.

"Looks like all kinds of vegetables in there!" Billy said. "I see garlic ... and tomatoes!" *This is just what I hoped for in my journal,* Billy remembered.

This is the meal I always imagined. I've only ever seen it through a window until now.

Mama Carol emerged from the back pantry. "Hello, children." They all dined and fellowshipped like they had known each other their whole lives. After dinner, Mama Carol showed the gang to their rooms and showed them where they could wash up.

"Say, chicken hawks," Reverend Timothy said, "tomorrow, come and find me when you're dressed and ready. I have something to show you."

The gang, excited, but too exhausted from the day's events, couldn't fight sleep any longer. They all retired to their rooms for the night for a deep deep sleep.

The Inexplicable Vine

The next morning, after breakfast, Reverend Timothy led the crew to the land behind his home. "Look at that *vine*!" Rosie said, skipping over to get a closer look. Rosie had always been drawn to plants. She wondered if perhaps her mom had been a plant-lover also, and if that were the reason she'd named her Rosie.

The vine was thick and brilliant green. "This isn't just any vine, chicken hawks," Reverend Timothy said. "This vine is the source of all power and comfort. Surely, you noticed animals at peace with each other and behaving differently than they do in the world—that's the result of the freedom and security they get from the inexplicable vine," he explained. "Here!" he said, handing Rosie a piece of fruit from the vine, "Have a taste!"

The gang watched Rosie to see what she thought of the fruit. "It's AMAZING!" Rosie said, mouth full of fruit. "It's a melon ... a peachy-melon! No, a PEAR! ... maybe a nectarine! Wow, it's delicious," she gushed. "What *is* it?" Rosie asked the reverend.

"That's just it," the Reverend answered. "We didn't plant the seed, and we don't tend the garden. This living brook keeps the vine constantly replenished with fresh water, but no river feeds into the brook," he said. "You look confused," he said, looking at the gang. "See, this vine supplies every nutrient we need for life, but it doesn't come from our labor," he said.

Reverend Timothy stepped to the left away from the flourishing garden and began again to speak. "See, here, chicken hawks," he said. "Mama Carol and I take good care of this garden. We water it, hoe the ground and spread fertilizer, but the fruit produces only in its season. And, when we have fruit, it's tart—almost too tart to bear—and of little nutritional value."

"What's he talking about?" Fredek whispered to Billy.

"Son," the reverend said, overhearing Fredek's comment, "When you worry and fret, when you hustle and strive in your own strength, God wants you to change gardens. Come to Him, where strivings cease and fruits grow in season and out as you seek the life of Jesus Christ. The garden we tend represents the self, but the flourishing garden is the life of God in us when we give our concerns to Him."

Reverend Timothy picked up a vine from each garden. "If you and your gang decide to produce fruit on your own, you could do it with enough sweat and worry. On the other hand, if you let God produce the fruit for you—His sons and daughters—God produces fruit in you and sustains it as you seek Him. Hebrews 11:6 tells us, "... *without faith it is impossible to please him: for he that cometh to God must believe that he is, and that he is a rewarder of them that diligently seek him.*"

Fredek Sheds His Nickname

"So, God is some kind of inexplicable vine?" Fredek asked, half excited and half skeptical.

"More than inexplicable," Reverend Timothy answered tenderly, "He's divine."

"I don't get it," Fredek continued. "If God makes *fruit* in our *garden* ... then what do I need with all this good living—manners, and not sinning and all of that?

"Who else wonders this?" the reverend asked the gang. They stared back at him. Finally, Billy lifted his hand.

"I guess I do," Billy confessed with a sheepish smile.

"Questions are good, young chicken hawks. Never fear your own questions. Jesus's followers asked so many questions—sometimes Jesus gave them straight answers, but most of the time, His answers were beyond their comprehension. But, still … they asked. And, you are wise to ask questions, too, son. *What is your name?*"

"Chubby," Fredek answered.

"Are you not Fredek?" Reverend Timothy asked.

"Well, …" Fredek said, wondering if Gabe had revealed his real name to Reverend Timothy, as well. "I *am*, but …"

"But, someone gave you a label that you agreed to carry." the reverend said.

"Yeah, I guess so," Fredek answered.

"And, are you ready to lay them down?" the reverend asked. Fredek didn't respond. "The labels the world placed on you," he continued.

Fredek nodded his head.

Reverend Timothy expounded: "You see Fredek in your name is the embodiment of who you are—your hopes, dreams, gifts, your legacy, your lineage … *everything!* The quickest way to get into trouble is to forget who you are. Or, worse, remember who you are and refuse to be it.

One of my former students got into a foolish land deal. You see, he forgot who he was and it cost him wasted time and money. And, son, time is something we can't ever get back this side of heaven. You know why he did it? Why he did the deal?" the reverend asked.

Fredek didn't answer.

"To get his step pa's approval," the reverend answered.

We're built to want to please our earthly fathers, but we only have one father—our Father in heaven. When our father on earth causes us pain or our friends call us names, it makes it hard to love them. But being a channel of God's love is the only way to be free, free to embrace your true name, Fredek. Be so careful not to let anything invade your heart that causes you to run from the person God made you to be.

Fredek nodded.

"I thought he *liked* 'Chubby,'" Anne said, surprised. Josey just smiled. Understanding the power of labels, she had never embraced Fredek's nickname.

"And, would you like to make it official?" the reverend asked, "—that you are the image bearer of Christ, blessed with a name by those who love you."

Fredek stood for a moment. He looked around at the smiling faces of the gang. He felt one swift pat on the back from Billy to his right. He looked down at the ground, then lifted his head. "I'm Fredek!" Fredek said quietly. "I'M FREDEK!" he repeated.

"You *are* Fredek, indeed—a young man of tremendous strength and courage; a peacemaker. Some may call you Fred, which means peaceful ruler," said Reverend Timothy.

This is the first time Fredek understood the meaning of his name. The chest inside his 6'4" stature swelled as the reverend described the man he was called to be, and for the first time in his life, he felt it was possible.

Life in the Vine

"Now, Fredek," the reverend began, "and all of you. It's true the fruit is produced without human effort, but that doesn't mean that one isn't to work. One must pick the fruit. One must allow God to prune the plant."

"Secondly," the reverend continued," As you rest, knowing God gardens the vine, you continue to steward your *mind* as you face problems, knowing the Father in Heaven is a trustworthy source of life and guidance. Grow in wisdom, knowledge, favor with God and favor with man, just as Jesus did (Luke 2:52, James 1:5). All the while, know that God will never leave or forsake you (Hebrew 13:5). He will provide all your needs according to His riches in glory (Philippians 4:19). He will fill your heart with peace."

The reverend paused and looked up to the sky. The gang watched to see what he might say next.

"See my beautiful wife, there, walking among the inexplicable vine?" the reverend asked. "One year ago, she and I lost our son—our only son— to tuberculosis. He was caring for wounded soldiers as a medic. They called him a *conscientious objector*—someone who wants to serve with courage but does not feel he can raise arms against his fellow man with a clear conscience. His loss brought intense grief to our hearts, but when we abide in the vine, our sadness melts like a candle releasing the sweet aroma of God's presence with us. That's what allows us to face each day in the midst of pain."

A tear fell down Josey's cheek as she listened. *How could Mama Carol trust in a God that allowed her son to die?* she wondered to herself. She thought about her own family—so many of them had lost their lives at the mercy of hateful hands. *Where was their rescuer?* She thought. Josey wanted to trust God's goodness, but sometimes she wondered whether God were too weak or too uncaring to stop evil.

A Letter for Lizzy

"Now, which one of you is Lizzy?" Reverend Timothy asked. Although, somehow everyone thought he knew the answer. Lizzy stepped forward. "Lizzy, Gabe gave me this letter for you."

Heavenly Father,

Thank you for our daughter Elizabeth Tanzer whom we call Lizzy and are humbled by the gift of life she is to us from you, the Creator of all life. We're blessed beyond measure.

We dedicate her wholly to you and ask that you grant her the spirit of wisdom and revelation that she may know You better just as Paul prayed for the Ephesians.

We pray she grows into a virtuous woman who walks not in the counsel of the wicked, nor stands in the way of sinners, nor sits in the seat of mockers, but that her delight would be in You daily as young David describes in the first Psalm.

We hope her heart will be filled with worship, knowing the Lord is her strength and song, and that He will become her salvation early in life. We pray that in her desperate moments, when we are not near, that she will fearlessly proclaim the words of Exodus 15:2, "The Lord is my strength and song, and he is become my salvation: he is my God, and I will prepare him a habitation; my Dad's God, and I will exalt him."

In Your time, Lord, lead her to a gentleman you would have for her that they may complement one another to fulfill Your purposes on this earth. Above all, we ask that she know You, the one true God, and Jesus Christ, whom you have sent as it is written in John 17:3, and that she would walk worthy of the Lord, being fruitful in every good work, and increasing in the knowledge of God, as Paul hoped for the Colossians.

We pray all of these things in the name of Jesus Christ.

Amen

Lizzy stood speechless—shocked to hear the love her parents had for her and their passion for her to know God.

"May I keep it?" Lizzy said, extending her little hand toward the reverend.

"Yes, Lizzy," Reverend Timothy answered. "Keep it close," he said.

Wake Up, Fredek!

The next norming was Sunday. The gang joined Mama Carol and Reverend Timothy in a church service held weekly for all of the families on the North River. About 150 people filled the small building.

Rascal led the way, heading for a front-row seat. "Whoa, whoa ... where you headed there, Rascal?" Fredek asked. "We don't want to take the good seats, after all. Let's take this row right here," he said, pointing to the rear-most row in the sanctuary.

"In the back?" Rascal said. "Well, sure, I suppose," he agreed.

The boys funneled into the back row, while the girls made themselves comfortable one row ahead. The reverend launched into a rather lively message with a good helping of exclamations mixed with silent pauses. It was one of those pauses that lulled Fredek right into a deep sleep.

Billy, noticing Fredek's stage, nudged Rascal with a firm elbow and gestured toward their sleeping neighbor. By this time, a stream of drool had formed down one side of Fredek's face. Without speaking, Billy alerted Rascal to hand him a hymnal. With maximum stealth and silence, Billy gently tore a page from the hymnal. "Watch this," he whispered to Rascal, being sure not to be heard by the girls in front of them. Billy rolled up the hymnal page like a cigar and lodged it right in the corner of Fredek's mouth. Rascal and Billy could hardly restrain their laughter. With noses plugged and mouths covered, somehow, they managed to bind up their outbursts.

Just then, Reverend Timothy made one last call for testimonies. "If all minds are cleared, let us turn to page 123 in your hymnal to join our voices in 'Amazing Grace' before dismissing," he invited.

"Fredek, FREDEK!" Billy said as he elbowed him. "The reverend wants you to sing a song so we can get out of here!" he said.

Fredek roused and jumped up to disguise the fact of his slumber. Before he'd fully awakened, he was already belting out verse one. ... *that saved a wretch like ME!* he sang boldly. Fully coming to, Fredek realized no one else was singing. In fact, no one else was even standing.

He stopped singing to see the mothers covering their children's eyes. He patted himself to see what they might be staring at. *Is my hair a mess?* he wondered. Then, he felt it—a giant paper cigar glued to his bottom lip with drool.

"Well, young chicken hawk," said Reverend Timothy. "I think I speak for all of us when I say thank you for that memorable verse. Now, if you wouldn't mind closing us in prayer," he said, smiling.

Fredek thanked God for His provisions, and church was dismissed. The boys laughed all the way back to the cottage, but the girls were much less than amused. Lucky for Fredek, the pity the girls had for him caused them to be extra nice for the rest of the day.

Back at the cottage, the gang had a peaceful night's sleep.

"Tomorrow ... Pleasant Valley," Billy said to the boys in his room.

"Pleasant Valley, indeed," a voice said.

"Gabe?" Billy said in a whisper, looking around for their friend who was nowhere to be seen. "Oh, Gabe," Billy muttered, with a smile and a shake of the head.

Ask Yourself

1. Using parts of a wagon, how could you build a raft to travel a river?
2. What's the importance of teamwork? How does grumbling affect the team? The leader? The followers?
3. How is it possible for Christians to respond differently than the world when they face the loss of a loved one? (I Thessalonians 4:13)
4. Do you believe in guardian angels? Why is it important to be hospitable around strangers? (Hebrews 13:2)
5. Josey wondered if God were weak or uncaring. What do you wonder about God that might cause you not to trust Him? When bad things happen—like separation from loved ones or broken trust—what does the Bible promise? (Psalm 23)
6. What do you think the letter from Lizzy's parents meant to her? How do you think the letter might affect her as she grows up? If an angel could deliver a letter from your parents, what do you wish it would say?

Outdoor Survival tips: S.T.O.P. (I'm LOST!)

Even experienced explorers get lost. If this happens to you, S.T.O.P. First, simply **STOP**: don't panic. **THINK**: Where did I come from, and what's ahead? If possible, return back to a familiar location. **OBSERVE**: Look at land markers and traces you left along your path. Check for clues like the suns position and your position relative to mountains or ravines. While you still have sunlight, take note of potential shelters without departing too far from your original route. **PLAN**: Consider the above factors. Take action to stay hydrated with clean water and alert others with a whistle. Then, make a wise plan. As a last resort, follow the path of a creek or river. You may not know where it will lead, but you will move in a constant direction. Avoid canyons that pose danger of falling rock and sudden floods. Finally, heed this warning: Never float downstream at night or in dense fog, as the stream may flow off a cliff without warning!

Follow Billy's Journey

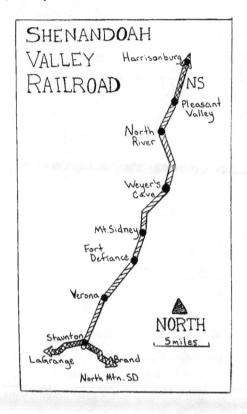

Chapter Nine

Pleasant Valley, Virginia

The Cryptic Piano

Dear Ma and Pa,

This letter comes to you by candlelight somewhere along the North River. I wonder sometimes if you have any knowledge of these letters since you've gone ahead of me to eternity, but even if you don't, it gives me comfort to share these amazing adventures with you.

I wonder if from eternity you can see a broader dimension of my life. Or, maybe there's too much going on up there to notice. The adventures down here are stranger than I ever expected—talking animals and inexplicable vines and all. I just don't understand why those otters would be curmudgeonly when they know about the life of the vine. And, how come the first wolf we saw was ferocious, but the second wolf rested so peacefully with the baby rabbits?

I suppose all of us creatures have a choice to make—to receive love or reject it. Maybe that's what Reverend Timothy was trying to teach us with those vines.

121

I sure can't wait to ask God all of these things when I see you again.

Love to you both,
Billy

You'll See

The overcast sky caused the gang to sleep through dawn 'til half-past seven 'o clock. In the span of five minutes, the gang roused and rearranged their bedding back into the pristine conditions of Mama Carol's hospitality.

One by one, each traveler found his seat at the breakfast table. All were accounted for except Rosie. "She probably has her head in a book," Lizzy said. "I'll fetch'er," she added.

Lizzy returned with a sluggish but smiling Rosie in tow. "Yep, she was up all-night reading—just as I suspected," Lizzy said, directing Rosie to her chair.

Reverend Timothy led the gang in a prayer of thanksgiving for the day's provisions. Before the reverend could say, "Amen," Fredek blurted out, "WOW, this JAM is amazing!"

Mama Carol, wishing to blow by the fact that Fredek indulged before the table had finished saying grace, held back a chuckle. "Oh, the jam. I'm glad you like it!" Pulling back a white linen towel to reveal a heap of steaming biscuits, Mama Carol took one for herself, then passed the basket to her right. "Biscuit?" she offered. "Now, Fredek, would you pass the inexplicable jam?"

"Inexplicable jam?" Fredek said with excitement. "You mean this is from that inexplicable vine?"

Smiling, Mama Carol answered, "Wye, of course, son. The vine's blessings are for all who would partake."

"Maybe *that's* why I feel like a giant!" he said, tilting his chin up like a statue.

"You *are* a giant!" Billy interjected, referring to Fredek's commanding stature.

"You'll see," Fredek said, gesturing to Billy to taste the jam.

Everyone dined on the fresh biscuits and jam. "LOOK," Rascal exclaimed, "I don't even *need* these!" he said, removing his bifocals. "I can see!"

Giggling, Mama Carol explained, "This strength should last most of the day, little ones. You'll need it."

"Looks like Rosie is perking up, too," Lizzy said, noting how the inexplicable jam had revived her sleepy friend.

Mama Carol looked at Timothy seated to her left. "Why are you smiling, my love?" he asked, knowing the answer. He had seen her light up before as she witnessed people appreciating the fruits of the vine. She smiled and turned back toward the children.

The gang laughed and ate until their bellies were full to the neck. Everyone abounded in energy as they boarded the raft. Mama Carol bid them farewell with a large pack of salted meat and a jar of inexplicable jam for every traveler.

"Wye, thanks!" Billy said, as he received the gifts.

"Write often, and be kind," the reverend said.

"And, you watch your manners, gentlemen," Mama Carol called, waving.

A New Gift

The gang pushed away from the bank with one collective shove. Billy couldn't help but think back to Gabe's letter. He'd been trying to avoid the thought ever since he had read it, because the thought only spurred anxiety. *What is my gift? Should I know by now?* He wondered. *How can I use it to help the group if I don't even know what it is?*

Perhaps Billy mumbled some of his thoughts out loud, because Anne turned to him and said, "What are you muttering about, Billy?"

He almost snarked back, but something stopped him. *Be kind,* he thought. *Reverend Timothy said be kind. Is kindness a super power?* he wondered as he wound the tethering rope and packed it away. Billy wasn't sure if he'd found his super power, but he figured he'd exercise it anyway.

The raft floated securely down the river under an ever-darkening sky. The fresh smell in the air just before a storm always took Billy back to happy days of his childhood. "Rain's a'comin'," he alerted.

Sure enough, the clouds thickened, and the winds picked up creating rapids the gang weren't sure the raft could handle. Anxiety hit the gang, so much so, that Fredek found himself a bit confused. "Now, I'm new to this God thing, sure, but didn't that Jesus man speak to storms?"

Just then, everything grew calm. The gang paused from their efforts to secure the supplies and looked up at the sky. "Is it over?" Rascal said.

The words barely left his mouth before in a nanosecond a white snake-like cloud burst down from a dark wall in the sky. It let forth a menacing whistle as it uprooted a patch of young trees, leaving behind nothing more than a dirt patch. When the rogue cloud whipped up to the edge of the river, the gang cringed. They huddled together as the cloud seemed to turn and head right towards them.

Rosie screamed as the cyclone pulled her legs out from under her. The gang clung to her by hand, hair and shirt sleeves to keep her on the raft. "Lord, lord!" Billy shouted. The cloud lifted the clump of travelers off of the raft. Billy peaked through a slit in his eyelids. "Jesus!" he whispered.

Silence. One by one the gang unclenched their eyes and their grip on Rosie. "ROSIE!" Lizzy yelled out, embracing Rosie forcefully. "Rosie, I thought we lost you."

The travelers looked around. They watched the exchange with Lizzy and Rosie but were too discombobulated to say anything, themselves, just yet.

Finally, Rascal spoke. "Where ... *are* we?"

Billy, coming to his senses, realized something amazing. The gang was an hour ahead in their journey—safe and sound with all of their supplies and pets in a small, dry room in Pleasant Valley (an hour's journey down the river from where they'd been picked up). *Translocation!* Billy thought. *That's it!*

"I think, ... I think this is Pleasant Valley," Billy said. "I think the Lord heard my cry and brought us here," he said. "Translocation and all."

The gang looked at him in a stupor. "Well, I'm just happy to be alive—trans … uh, muhnition or not!" Fredek exclaimed. "Thank you, God, for saving us!"

"I see four rooms," Josey said, "but no door. How do we get out of here?" The small living room between the four living quarters was lit with candles positioned next to a fireplace with no firewood. There was no door to be seen, but on the floor lay an invoice for five days in an inn—marked "paid in full."

"This must be an inn—some sort of hotel. And, it looks like someone paid our way!" Anne said, examining the invoice.

"But Josey has a point," Fredek said, "There must be a way out." Lizzy, wiping the tears from her eyes, stood up and bumped a candle stand with her elbow.

"It's opening!" Josey said, pointing to a passage way now visible through the fireplace. The gang walked through the opening into a secret room. Inside, they found a piano.

Anne, an accomplished pianist, took no time to sit at the shiny instrument and begin to play. The words "Joe & Doris Vogt" were inscribed into the fall board—the flat part just below the music rack. "Aren't you related to some Vogts?" Anne asked, remembering once when Billy had mentioned his real name.

Anne stood up, so Billy could take a closer look. "Those are my great grandparents!" he said. The gang was amazed. They surrounded the piano wondering just what it all meant. "Listen," Billy said, "I think it's playing."

The gang listened as the sound grew and the keys depressed with no visible pianist at the keys. "I know that song," Lizzy said. "It is well, it is well with my soul," she sang.

Billy's heart was bursting. He'd finally identified the gift God had given him and used it to move his friends out of harm's way. He felt like God was sending him a personal letter to let him know he wasn't on this journey alone. Billy crumbled to his knees, head in his hands, and said a few quiet words of thanks.

Anne explored the piano further. Inside, she found an old stick of bright red lipstick and several sheets of music. "Smells like old woman," Anne said, waving her hand in front of her nose, "Oh! Ludwig Van Beethoven," she said, glowing. "This is my favorite," she commented, as she turned the first page. "Oh, look. Your Grandmother Doris has written something:"

> *To my grandboys:*
> *May music always walk with you on the path of life like a friend*
> *you cannot shake. May its words comfort your souls and its rhythms*
> *remind you of unexpected love.*
> *With love,*
> *Grandfather Joe & Grandmother Doris*

"Wow, a letter," said Billy. He took hold of the yellowed paper and reread it quietly. The aroma of soured perfume was strong but strangely comforting.

"Weren't you the only grandson?" Anne asked.

"As far as I know, yeah," Billy answered. "I must have some cousins out there or something. Who knows!"

The Inn: Night One

Rascal, who had disappeared while the piano played, resurfaced. "I found a way out," he said. Rascal reopened a door he'd found and led the gang through a corridor that spilled out into a town restaurant.

"Pleasant Valley Restaurant," Fredek read. "Sounds good to me!" he said. The hungry gang nominated Rascal to approach a gentleman behind the counter to see about food pricing.

Rascal returned, "Well, it looks like someone knew we were coming again."

"What?" Billy said.

"Five days of hot meals coming up!" Rascal revealed. Smiles filled every face. The gang selected a table and filled the benches. The owner served a hot roast and large bowl of mashed potatoes, family style, making sure the animals had their fill of scraps. The filling meal settled the gang after a challenging day on the river and was just what they needed before a good night's sleep. They made their way back through the corridor, through the secret room and into the small living area where they had started. From there, they divvied up the four separate sleeping quarters and settled in for the night.

The next morning, the boys traveled back to the restaurant to find someone in charge of the inn. They found a clerk—a handsome young man, full of life and energy (like he'd eaten a fresh spoonful of inexplicable jam, in fact). He introduced himself as Joey Carlton and described big dreams he had to change the world for good and how he wasn't quite sure how he was going to go about it. It was more of a stirring inside of him.

"Listen, you all are new to town. I'll show you around," Joey offered. "I finish here around supper time and will meet you just out front," he said.

The boys were keen on the idea. They agreed and returned to inform the girls.

That evening, the gang met Joey in front of the restaurant as planned. "It's so nice of you to show us around," Anne said.

"Well, it's nothing more than others have done for me." Having heard Joey's stories that morning, the boys could tell the clerk was already in storytelling mode, "You see, last summer, my Father and I traveled to Italy where we met a man named Guglielmo Marconi. He offered to show *us* around, since my family didn't know a word of Italian except My Father. That man had a heart for inventions and an interest in wireless telegraphy— sound waves that travel through the air, you see. I have a feeling he'll make it work, someday," Joey predicted. "Either he will, ... or *me and my Father will*," he added boldly.

Billy leaned over to Rascal, "This fella's either insane or brilliant."

Rascal laughed. "Time will tell," he said. "At least he's dreaming," Rascal said.

Rascal's comment struck Billy in the heart. *I'm dreaming, too.* He thought, defensively. But, then he wondered, *Do I really have a dream— something that's driving me?* He thought about communicating through invisible waves. *If that ever happens, we can speak of all of the goodness of*

God, and people can hear it across the world. That would be a great dream, he thought.

The gang returned to the inn and washed up before supper in the restaurant. At the table, Billy told the gang about a story he remembered reading in his dad's Bible. "People remember David and Goliath, but they forget about all of the other giants David and his men conquered," Billy said.

"Listen to this, Billy said, as he opened his Pa's Bible to I Chronicles 20:5-6"

And there was war again with the Philistines; and Elhanan the son of Jair slew Lahmi the brother of Goliath the Gittite, whose spear staff was like a weaver's beam.

And yet again there was war at Gath, where was a man of great stature, whose fingers and toes were four and twenty, six on each hand, and six on each foot and he also was the son of the giant.

"Can you believe there were a bunch of giants on the earth during Bible times?" Billy said, with the excitement of a child. "What if the orange-eyed creature was a descendent of those giants?" he said.

"Giants?" Josey said—part of her wondered if it were possible.

Rascal chimed in, "What if the spear, or … what did you call it? A weaver's beam? What if that is what my knife actually is…wow!"

Billy had intended to encourage the group with these retellings of the giants David and his men slew, but as he read, he noticed Lizzy's head drop in shame. He made his way to her and said, "Is everything okay, Lizzy?"

"I guess I'm just one of those six-toed monsters," Lizzy sobbed. "I'm cursed."

"Now, you just wait a moment, there, sister," Billy said firmly. "There is no curse on you. There is nothing in the heart or the body that God can't call good if you let Him."

"Is that true?" Lizzy asked. "Even a sixth toe?"

"Oh, especially that. That's an easy one!" Billy said, smiling like a big brother. Lizzy took comfort in his words and for the first time felt comfortable in the skin God gave her.

Milton

After the gang finished dinner and an hour or so of stories, they stood up to return to their rooms. "Wye, evening, young squires," a man greeted. A healthy-looking man in his 60s approached the gang. "My apologies, but I could not help but hear your most riveting conversation," he said. "My name is Milton. And where are your parents this evening?" he asked.

Sensing trouble, Anne piped up with an untruth. People had asked this before, and it always bore fear in the hearts of the children who wondered whether they'd be sent back or placed in an overcrowded local orphanage. "Well, sir," Anne began, "Our parents are upstairs in their room."

"Oh, wonderful," Milton replied. He wasn't sure he'd been told the truth. "And, where is this fine bunch of young ladies and gentlemen heading?" he asked.

"We're going to Harrisonburg," Anne stated.

"—to visit my Aunt!" Billy added abruptly. "To visit my Aunt Sunny," he repeated, relieved to be able to actually tell the truth.

"Do you mean Mrs. Sunny Vogt?" Milton asked intently.

"You know my Uncle John and Aunt Sunny?" Billy said, stunned.

"Wye, I certainly do," Milton said, as he seated himself at the table the gang had just vacated and proceeded to light his pipe, as if settling in for a long chat. "Sunny was my first girlfriend in college, but religious differences prompted our separation. She attended Assemblies of God, while I had grown up in a Roman Catholic monastery. I remember what a beautiful and charming speaker she was," he said. "I spoke with her just last year, in fact, at an event for retired educators where we discussed politics and pleasantries," Milton recalled as he took another puff on the pipe.

"I can't believe you know her," Billy said.

"Oh, indeed," Milton responded with glee. "Apart from her lovely blue eyes, I remember her collection."

"Her collection?" Billy asked.

"Yes, she had a passionate affinity for collecting thimbles," Milton said. Billy looked confused, "Wye, you know, son—those metal cuffs worn to protect the fingertip of a lady during her sewing tasks."

"Oh, sure. Of course, I've seen a thimble," Billy assured.

"I thought the perfect thimble might incline Sunny's heart toward me," Milton continued. "I didn't have much money, but I had endeared myself to a local seamstress with whom I had been paying in warm bread rather than coins. One day, when I entered to deliver trousers in need of repair, the seamstress gifted me her oldest thimble. I knew instantly I would gift it to Sunny."

Josey, Rosie, Lizzy and Anne listened intently to the forming love story. "The thimble was so worn by time and labor that holes had formed in the metal. Growing up as an orphan, the thimble reminded me of the holes I always had in my socks and shoes. The memories filled me with shame that almost caused me not to give her the thimble. Nevertheless, the next day, when I met Sunny for lunch, I slid it across the table to her."

"What did she *say?*" the girls said, almost in unison.

"Sunny asked me to tell her the story of the thimble, which I did," Milton said. "Then she said, 'Milton, this is the most beautiful thimble in my collection, and it proves two things—the great care the seamstress had for her work and for her family.'

As Milton recounted the story, a tear welled up in his eye. "She saw beauty and virtue in that old gift. What a dear woman," he said, taking another puff of his pipe.

Josey, checked the thimble around her neck and found it glowing for the first time in a long time. "Do you have any regrets?" she asked the man.

"Regrets?" Milton said. "Oh, no regrets—only wonders. I *did* often wonder if I should have focused on our commonalities more than our differences," he said. "Do me a favor, would you?" he asked. "Send my best regards," he said.

The gang bid the man a good night and parted. "Tomorrow," Billy said, "Harrisonburg!"

Ask Yourself

1. What do you think about God removing the gang from a dangerous situation? Does God still work that way? (see Acts 8:26-40, Philip and the Ethiopian)
2. James had dreams for his life. How do you think that will affect his decisions in life?
3. Anne deceived Milton. Why did she do this? Would you have done the same thing?
4. Milton's memories made him feel like he and his gift were inadequate. How do you think those feelings impacted his actions? Do you ever have times when you have to choose actions that don't line up with your feelings?

Outdoor Survival Tips: Tornado Precautions

A tornado *watch* means conditions are right for tornadoes to form; whereas a tornado *warning* means a tornado is on the ground (take cover!). The safest places are basements and underground shelters. If you are outdoors, get inside a sturdy building; otherwise, lie down low in a ditch or low-lying area with your arms over your head and neck for protection. Low areas may flood or be home to poisonous snakes, so stay alert!

Follow Billy's Journey

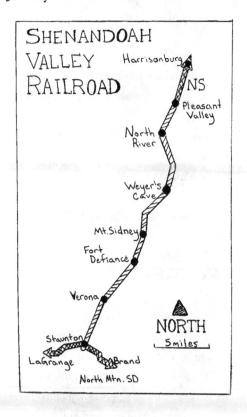

Chapter Ten

Harrisonburg, Virginia

The Mystery of Aunt Sunny

Dear Ma and Pa,

Back in Ladd, my teacher, Mrs. Morey taught us about unrequited love. She said it's when you love someone who doesn't love you back. That sounds a lot like Mr. Milton and Aunt Sunny, to me. But, you probably already know that story.

Tomorrow, we arrive at Harrisonburg by train—exceptin' we get caught. But, we're plenty careful about that. We washed up and put on our best clothes for the trip. That usually helps ease the suspicion of grown folk.

Pa, thinking about what we might have done together makes me sad. We would have had fun playing baseball and catching fish. I sure could use a little help on my arithmetic, but I don't suppose that's fun.

I wonder if Aunt Sunny has remarried. I wonder if he plays baseball ... or drinks like Uncle John.

All my love,

Billy

133

A Ticket to Ride

The gang considered remaining in Pleasant Valley for the entire five days for which someone had prepaid their stay, but the anticipation of Harrisonburg was too much to deny. The morning after the gang met Milton—a former admirer of Aunt Sunny's—they decided to begin the last leg of the journey.

"I'll get the tickets," Billy said. "James told me there's only one train out on Wednesdays, and it leaves at high noon." The gang decided to enjoy a morning meal in the restaurant while Billy purchased tickets for their journey. "Be sure to wear your fine clothes today—the ones from the monastery. Looking unkempt will only draw unwanted attention," Billy reminded.

Billy returned within the hour, and the gang made their way to the station. "Billy," Rascal said in a low voice, "Did you see those?" Rascal pointed to dozens of posters headlined in large black letters that read: MISSING.

"Think we're up there?" Billy said, trying to seem confident. He saw the concern on Rascal's face. "You know, Rasc. There are hundreds of children out on their own these days—orphans, former slaves and just plain 'ol independent-minded men, like myself. I'm not worried," Billy said. He gave Rascal a pat on the back as they continued to the train.

After the war, the treatment of former slaves was inconsistent. Josey, unsure who and what she might encounter, always kept a document with her. It was barely legible, having traveled in her bag for a few years, but it verified that her family's work supported the Confederacy.

The Fugitive Slave Act in 1850 required the return of runaway slaves, but by August 1861, the United States Congress and the Union Army began classifying found slaves as "Contraband," which allowed runaways to remain (not be returned to their owners), live freely and be paid for their labors.

The newfound freedom paved the way for new communities—first in the development of "Contraband" camps, then in the formation of a powerful force against the Confederacy: The United States Colored Troops

(USCT). The USCT formed in 1863 under the umbrella of the United States Army and made up about ten percent of the Union forces. This voluntary force played an important role in bringing the Civil War to a close and abolishing slavery forever.

Such heroic deeds took place during the American Civil War that a new medal was created: The Medal of Honor. During the War, 25 colored men received this high honor—15 USCT soldiers and ten Union Navy soldiers.

Despite all these developments, Josey was cautious around new people. A large man directed her to a table where colored people were presenting documentation. Her heart pounded in her chest, but the warmth of her glowing thimble gave her strange comfort.

Anne stood back, bothered that Josey had been separated from the gang. Billy stood in close proximity to Anne in her frustration, just in case he needed to keep her from hauling off a closed fist at someone.

Josey's papers satisfied the station official (along with a story she'd told about her caretakers being on the next train), and she rejoined the gang. On the train, the gang ushered Josey to a corner by the window with her friends around her at every angle, to help her feel comfortable around so many strangers.

The chug of the engine ignited everyone's imagination. Lizzy imagined how beautiful Aunt Sunny must be (based on Mr. Milton's stories of her). Billy imagined her surprise to see him and the way she might run at him with open arms.

Before they knew it, they had arrived. Debarking the train, the gang was unsure where to start. "After all of this travel, what now?" Billy said, chuckling. The crowd was dense with ladies and gentlemen focused on their own schedules, which was fine with Billy. "If they're focused on themselves, they're not focused on us. And that's a *good* thing!" Billy said to the gang.

Billy always became chatty when his nerves got to him, and only his close friends knew that. Rascal came up beside him and asked, "You okay, Billy?"

Billy, about to tell another joke, paused and smirked, knowing Rascal could see right through him. "I suppose, well … I might have a batch of nerves," he said. "Part of me knows Aunt Sunny will welcome us with a happy heart, but another part of me wonders if this was all a fool's errand," Billy confessed.

Billy quieted just long enough for his eyes to fill with tears. Rascal had never seen Billy like this. Anne kept an eye on this exchange but gave the boys their space. "It's just—" Billy said, straightening up, "It's just the thought of being wanted, of being loved. When I think of it, it nearly knocks me over," Billy said. Rascal understood completely.

Aunt Sunny—Beautiful and Mysterious

A woman stepped out from the crowd with a sign reading: WILLIAM & FRIENDS.

"Billy, is it her?" Anne asked.

"How did she know to meet us here?" Billy said. "More than that, how did she know I wasn't alone?"

Having not seen Aunt Sunny in several years, Billy chose to observe her for a few minutes to make sure it was really her.

The woman was stately and refined. "She looks like a queen," Rosie said. She wore a cream-colored dress decorated with red cherry detailing. It had a fitted bodice, high neck and wide skirt buttressed with a petticoat. Her hat was fine, like those of the ladies around her, and featured lace and roses made of ribbon.

A short coat of silk and cotton covered her shoulders and matched her fingerless gloves. Her mitts extended to her elbow with peaked flaps over the knuckles. The brass buckles glistened on her heeled leather shoes. *She does look like a queen,* Billy thought.

She must have noticed Billy staring, because she approached him and said, "William, is that you?"

"Aunt Sunny?" he said.

Aunt Sunny put her hand on Billy's face and looked into his blue eyes. She kissed his forehead and said, "William, my sweet nephew, you're a grown man. So, handsome! We've been waiting for you."

"Are these the friends we've been hearing about?" Aunt Sunny moved through the gang, embracing each person like family.

"They are," Billy said. "I don't understand how you knew we were coming," he said.

"Come with me," Aunt Sunny summoned with charm. "It's quite crowded here. Let's get you home."

The gang were captivated by her invitation, and they followed her eagerly. Aunt Sunny led the gang to two luxurious carriages waiting at the station's entrance. "Eric, would you mind helping our guests with their luggage," Sunny requested.

A 20-minute carriage ride carried the gang to the outskirts of Harrisonburg. Billy was getting used to the fact that the Aunt Sunny sitting in front of him wasn't the quaint midwife he'd imagined, but she was warmer and more welcoming than he expected.

Aunt Sunny explained that after the War, she transitioned from midwifery to nursing care. She recounted that one evening, after a long day of supporting surgeons in the hospital, she returned to the home that she and Uncle John shared. There, she found a certified letter at the doorstep. Inside, she found documentation declaring her the oldest living descendent of the Gibleigh Family Trust. "My family had wealth I never knew of," she said. "I inherited a large sum of gold-backed currency, a stack of railroad stock and 1,225 acres of river-bottom farmland plus the equipment and cattle (more than 1,100 head) to fill it.

The carriages slowed on the grounds of a grand estate where the gang was greeted by a tailor, seamstress, etiquette trainer and dance master. Aunt Sunny introduced these experts to the gang.

"These experts will prepare you for a fine Victorian Ball to occur in the coming months to celebrate your arrival," Sunny said. "Anne, we would be honored if you could prepare a piano piece to perform."

Anne grinned from ear to ear. "A ball? A *performance?!* I'd be absolutely honored," she said. "I have just the piece," she added, thinking of "Fur Elise," the beloved song of her teacher Lady Kathryn.

"Lizzy, this is Victor, a skilled vocal instructor. He's ready to prepare you to perform a song if you're willing," Aunt Sunny said.

Lizzy hesitated, "Oh, I've never—"

"Of *course,* she's willing!" Rosie answered.

"Well, this will be wonderful!" Aunt Sunny exclaimed, pressing her hands together like a prayer. "Eric, please show our guests to their rooms," she asked her footman.

Sunny stepped out of the carriage and entered the house. Anne blurted out from the carriage, "How do you know so much about us?"

Sunny turned. "Oh, dear ones. I've had my eye on you," she said as she continued into the house.

"That woman is as mysterious as she is beautiful," Anne said to the gang.

The Big Question

The gang joined Aunt Sunny for an early dinner. Afterward, she invited Billy to her private library to talk. Billy jumped right in.

"Aunt Sunny," Billy started. "Seems strange, but you've known my family longer than I have." Sunny smiled. "So, I wonder if you might be able to answer questions that I cannot."

"What questions do you have, William?" Aunt Sunny asked.

"You can call me Billy," Billy said.

"Okay. Billy," she said.

"Well, I know my mother died giving birth to me, and I just wonder, I guess, whether my dad—" Billy thought for a moment, "Well, whether he would have had it shake out another way, I guess."

"You mean, you wonder if your dad would have preferred to lose you and save your mother?" Aunt Sunny asked.

"I suppose so," Billy said.

"Oh, Billy," Aunt Sunny began. "The answer is complex, but it's also simple," she said. "You are created in the image of God. So are your friends for that matter. Your father wanted desperately to save you both, but you were chosen even before that," she said.

Billy looked up.

"See," Aunt Sunny continued. "God chose you to rest in His son Jesus no matter the situation in which you find yourself. You saw the inexplicable vine, right?"

Billy nodded.

"Well, that vine is symbolic of the divine rest and healing we embrace when we trust in Jesus through all things bad and good. The fruit produced is described in Galatians 5—namely love, joy, peace, patience, kindness, goodness, faithfulness, gentleness and long suffering. All of these we pour out to others to be a glimpse of God's perfect kingdom to them," said Aunt Sunny. "See, the Apostle Paul encouraged the church at Ephesus, like I'm encouraging you now. He said in Ephesians chapter 1 and verse 4 that God chose you before the foundation of the world. No human can change that," she said.

Billy was relieved to finally get that question off of his chest. He wanted to believe Aunt Sunny, but after twelve years of questioning himself, it was going to take some time.

"Billy, my attorney has done some work for me in preparation for your visit," Aunt Sunny said. "I wonder if you might want to consider something," she said. "I'm prepared to adopt you—"

"You mean live *here?*" Billy interrupted. "What about Rascal? And, the others are so far from home. What would they—"

"Billy," Aunt Sunny said calmly. "I'm prepared to adopt all of you—animals and all—well, after your friends search out their own family members if they wish," she said.

Billy was quiet. *Is this really happening?* he thought to himself. *Is she waiting on me to answer?* he wondered.

Sensing Billy was still unsure whether he could trust her, Aunt Sunny spoke to him transparently, "Billy, your father knew your mother long before you were conceived. I'm certain he would have wanted to grow old by her side. He loved her dearly, and he had never met you. It makes sense that you would wonder who he might choose."

The approach worked. Billy's defenses lowered as he listened.

"I want you to remember something. The Lord puts air in our lungs and holds our souls in life. We exercise free will in this world and do our best to make God's kingdom present, but we also recognize that it will not be fully present until the Lord returns and brings everything into perfect order. Until then, there is pain, but we are not alone in it," Aunt Sunny said.

Billy suddenly remembered that this delicate woman dressed in fine garments is the same woman who suffered for years in a home with an unpredictable man haunted by the evils of addiction. At once, empathy opened his heart to the powerful hope with which his Aunt Sunny spoke.

Just then, Rascal, who had been exploring the property, entered the room. "Oh, excuse me," Rascal said.

"Not at all, Rascal," Aunt Sunny said. "You're right on time. Have a seat!"

Slightly confused, Rascal smiled and took a seat in a separate chair near Billy. "Gentlemen," Aunt Sunny began, "Life has left you without family as the world defines it, but you have found it in each other, haven't you." The boys glanced at each other with a quick smirk then back at Sunny. "As you know, I assisted many mothers in delivery during my years as a midwife and nurse, and one of the mothers I assisted was yours, Rascal," she said.

"Really?" he said.

"Truly," Aunt Sunny answered. "I held your birth certificate on which your name was declared 'Garrett Daniel,' "she said, "which means 'rules by the spear' your mother told me." Rascal listened intently. He'd been told that his documents were lost long ago. It had never occurred to him to question his own name. "And, Billy, as you know, your mother told me that your name means 'determined protector.' "Billy nodded. "What you might not know is that all of this happened on the same day."

The boys smiled to learn that they shared a birthday. "I could have guessed!" Billy said. "We're basically twins!"

"Billy," Aunt Sunny said, realizing the boys didn't understand what she meant. "You are fraternal twins. You are brothers."

Billy stopped. "What ... *how*—" He didn't know what to say.

"On the day you were born, we suspected your mother might be carrying twins. She had grown so large that it had become hard for her to stand. We quickly knew that labor was taking a toll on her weak body. The doctor needed to perform an emergency Caesarean Section to protect the baby, but it meant your mother lost a lot of blood. I'll never forget the moment your mother looked at me and said, 'This is my work—to deliver these children to the world.' Then, she turned to me and continued, 'And, this is your work, Sunny, to receive them safely.' She knew she wouldn't survive labor. I committed to keep a distant eye on you two as you grew," Aunt Sunny explained. "You parents couldn't remain with you on earth, but God places orphans at the front of the line," she said, "and stays with them always."

"I don't understand how we were separated," Billy said. "Rascal spent his life in an orphanage, while I was cleaning up after Uncle John. I don't know which was worse."

"I don't either," Rascal said.

"You both lived with your father until age three. At that point, your father was called away to war, so the state mandated that you two live with your Uncle John. He and I were already separated at that point, and the stress of two small children along with the troubles of wartime only increased his destructive habits. His depression grew and grew until one day a nun requesting alms for the orphanage approached John in town. He had nothing to donate, but the encounter planted the seed in his imagination. He convinced himself you would be better off in a facility and planned to turn over *both* of you to their care. But, ultimately, he thought the larger of you two might grow into a sturdy help around the property. So, he delivered Garrett Da—" she stopped herself. "Um rather, I mean, *you*, Rascal. He delivered *you* to the doorstep of the orphanage and continued with life as usual. I suspect he battled intense guilt after that, because townsfolk told me he hardly left home."

Billy didn't know what to say. It seemed to be only by a fluke that he didn't end up in an orphanage. He felt both grateful and rejected all at the same time. Aunt Sunny leaned in close to both boys. "Young men, apart from Jesus, it is hard to shake rejection—maybe impossible," she said. Once again, she had read their minds.

"Do you remember when you were close to that magnificent vine in the North River? Do you remember the peace you felt? Do you remember feeling complete freedom from rejection?" Aunt Sunny asked the boys.

"Yes," the boys both said. They looked at each other and laughed that they'd answered simultaneously.

"Twins, alright," Billy chuckled.

"Well, when you put your heart and trust completely on Jesus, you find help with your feelings of loneliness and rejection. Jesus is the vine that is always with you," Sunny said.

The Truth Behind the Thimble

Billy and Rascal caught up with the others who were still exploring the property. "Where have you fellas been?" Anne asked.

"Oh, just catching up with Aunt Sunny," Billy said. "She sure knows a lot about the family," he said.

"Man alive, did you see this garden?" Rosie exclaimed. She was the one who would appreciate such things. The gang headed Rosie's direction.

"Stay with me for a moment, Anne," Aunt Sunny said, touching Anne's elbow. "I believe you received a thimble collection along with an anonymous letter from your Aunt Tamara's best friend."

"I did," Anne said.

"As it should be," Sunny replied. "That letter was from me, and the thimbles have their own stories. You probably didn't know one of the thimbles belonged to Billy's mother, did you?"

"I didn't," Anne said. "I didn't know there was any connection at all."

"Billy's mother passed in childbirth; however, as the life faded from her body, she turned to her husband, Alan, told him she loved him and reminded him of those words from the Gospel of John chapter 15 and verse 5:

> I am the vine, ye are the branches: He that abideth in me, and I in him, the same bringeth forth much fruit: for without me ye can do nothing.

Moments later, Carol passed, leaving behind two motherless sons. When the last breath had left her body, the green thimble at her bedside—the one she had used to sew so many baby garments as her pregnancy progressed—began to glow in one thousand directions casting the image of a brilliant green vine on the walls and ceiling along with words that read, 'You can do nothing without Jesus.'

"I had no idea," Anne said, "but I don't remember a green thimble in the collection."

Josey, who had been listening in nearby, stepped closer. As she did, the thimble on her chest glowed with a powerful warmth and light. She wondered if she would ever find a suitable time to confess to Anne her possession of the thimble, and she was certain she needed to tell Anne the whole story before the big event.

"Josey," Aunt Sunny said with compassion in her voice, "I would say it's a miracle that you and Anne found each other. Wouldn't you?" "Yes," Josey said to Aunt Sunny.

In a more mysterious tone Aunt Sunny said, "well, I think you both have lots to talk about."

Anne looked at them both not understanding fully what she meant by that comment.

A Burning Secret

That night, the thimble around Josey's neck started to glow *Not nowwwww!* she thought. She thought she might be able to ignore it, but the glow intensified to the point it began to burn her just below the neck where it hid beneath her ruffled collar.

This is it, Josey realized. *I have to tell her the rest of the story.* "Anne," said Josey let's take a walk on the estate. After they began walking it took Anne a few paces to realize Josey was no longer with her.

"Whoa, what's the matter, Josey?" Anne said, realizing Josey had stopped behind her. Anne looked back to see Josey clasping something in her hand, right at her neckline. "Josey! Are you *okay?*" Anne shouted, starting to worry.

"Anne," Josey said. "Something has been with me a long time now, and now I've come to see why." Josey slowly unrolled her fingers that had been working so hard to trap the burning light coming from the thimble. Anne didn't know what to think.

"What's that?" Anne asked. Josey removed the chain from her neck and separated it completely from the thimble while Anne took steps toward her for a better view.

"This is yours," Josey said. Extending her hand toward Anne with the thimble glowing a calm steady light that no longer burned.

Anne looked up at Josey then put her index finger in the thimble and lifted the item up for awestruck examination. "It's beautiful! How did you get this?"

"I found this long before us friends found each other, Anne." Josey said. "It has lit my path more than I can say, and I pray it will light yours, as well." Josey's eyes welled up as she spoke. "I'm so grateful to bring it home. I could hardly stand hiding it from you. I've wondered something terrible if it might be the missing thimble in your collection, but I feared you might think I took it, like a common thief," Josey said.

"Oh, Josey. Never!" Anne replied. The two talked well past midnight about the collection and the symbolism of each thimble. Anne was surprised to find that Josey had brought the entire case of thimbles along—just in case the girls never returned to the pastor's estate. Josey felt lighter and truly content to see a treasure she had loved in the hands of its rightful new owner.

"The night I found Pastor Jim and Lisa's house in Verona, I discovered a small cottage in the Shenandoah Valley with a most delicious looking peach pie in the window, cooling in the summer breeze. From the window, I saw letters addressed to Sunny Vogt, so I imagine the property was one of yours. Well, I was starved, having skipped the evening meal to escape, and that pie called to me something fierce. Being the middle of the night, I slipped in through the window for a small portion of pie. There, on the kitchen table was a green thimble. I thought nothing of it at first, but then, I thought I saw it glow. Still, I ignored it so as to absquatulate with haste. But, when I turned to leave, it glowed so intently, I was sure it was glowing for me. I had to make a quick decision, so," Josey looked at the ground, "I took it. I took the thimble."

"What I learned carrying this thimble is that the message is for all with an orphan heart—not just those separated from their parents, but those who carry orphan hearts because of their separation from the Father of all, Jesus. We biological orphans are independent. We're savvy, and we think we don't need to trust, because we've known so many people who weren't worthy of it, but God brings us to the front and whispers in our hearts that He will provide," Josey said. "Anne, I'm sorry that my choice kept the thimble from reaching you."

"Josey," Anne said, "I'm so sorry you felt like you needed to hold this secret. There's nothing to forgive."

Billy and Rascal returned from the garden to find the thimble still glowing around Josey's neck. "Whoa there, I've seen that glow before," Billy said, surprised. "It led us to the Staunton train station a few months back." Billy looked at Josey, "Was that *you?*" Josey nodded.

The Proposition

Lizzy, Fredek and Rosie strolled up to the others. "I'm so glad you enjoyed the garden. Now, it seems everyone is here. I wonder if you might be interested in a proposition," Aunt Sunny announced. "As I've shared with the boys, I would be honored for all of you to be a legal part of my household—*my children!* Now, I know matters of this magnitude is not to be rushed, so many of you will want to take time to explore other options. That's wise! But," she continued, "I want you to know you are treasured, and every one of you would be a crowning jewel on this home."

The children, especially Rosie and Lizzy, glowed with excitement from their fidgety fingers to their sparkling eyes. "Furthermore," Aunt Sunny added, "my chief land developer, Don Wooden, approached me about working with you dear ones to develop churches and orphan care here and around the world. He's a man of faith who oversees all of my properties and has done well by the principle set forth in Colossians chapter 3 and verse 23:

And whatsoever ye do, do it heartily, as to the Lord, and not unto men;

"As such," Aunt Sunny continued, "he will help you serve orphans. Also, as a wise follower of Christ, he will disciple you in your walk with the Lord. Above all, he'll teach you to focus on one life at a time as you serve others. God knows and loves us as individuals—every person on a unique journey with unique gifts."

Billy's face showed his excitement but his incomplete satisfaction with Aunt Sunny's words. "I don't get it," he said.

"What is it?" Aunt Sunny asked.

"Well, how'd you know we were coming—down to the time and place of our arrival?" Billy asked.

A knock reverberated from the front door and the gang turned to see who had arrived. Eric, the butler, positioned by the front door, quickly greeted the guest before presenting him to the lady of the house. "Ladies and gentlemen, the gentleman Gabe calling," Eric announced.

The gang was shocked to see the familiar face and worried how Aunt Sunny might respond to the stranger following them to her estate.

"Gabe!" Aunt Sunny exclaimed. "So good of you to join me on such short notice."

Gabe turned to Billy and winked covertly. "It was no trouble at all," Gabe answered. "I flew right over as soon as I received your message," he said.

"I just realized, I don't believe I know where you live," Aunt Sunny said, inquisitively.

"Oh, I stay with my Father who lives over the mountains," Gabe answered.

Anne leaned over to Billy, "She knows him, alright, but she doesn't know the whole bag, it seems."

"That's just what I was thinking," Billy said. "She doesn't *know!*"

Rascal, hearing Anne and Billy's discourse, chimed in: "Adults don't see it. They have more clutter in their minds than we youngins," he said.

"You're sayin' they don't have room for the supernatural," Billy said. Rascal nodded silently, so as not to interrupt Aunt Sunny's words.

"Children, Gabe lives in the area. I met him in town this winter one day when I'd gone to stock up on supplies, and he was so helpful—everywhere I needed him to be with just the right tool. He told me a little of his family. His father travels all over the region and knows pretty much everyone, it seems," Aunt Sunny said, smiling at Gabe. "In conversation, we realized that he knew *you, Billy!* When I returned home that day, I feared I'd never see him again, but every few weeks, Gabe and I continued to run into each other. Each time, he updated me about your whereabouts, your plans to journey here and the others who joined you along the way. All of the information helped me pray for each step of your journey. One day, while Eric and I cleared snow from the front landing, the thought came to me to prepare this home for you and your fellow travelers," she said.

"Did you ever think about coming to get us? Or perhaps sending a coach to collect us?" Rascal asked, innocently.

"I did," Sunny answered. "I prayed for you constantly, but I also discussed options with my top staff. Both my property manager, Don, and his wife, Melinda, convinced me that this journey would help you see what you're capable of, and, from what I can see, it did just that." Aunt Sunny extended her arm across Rascal's back and patted his opposite shoulder.

Fredek piped up, which happened pretty predictably when hunger struck, "So, about supper?"

The gang chuckled.

"Oh, yes! *Of course!*" Aunt Sunny blurted, brushing her hand against her forehead. "The staff has prepared a scrumptious evening meal for us. Tonight, you'll retire to the staff quarters. Tomorrow, construction!"

"Construction?" Billy said.

"Construction! A boy's home and a girl's home," Aunt Sunny repeated, resolutely. "But for now, take a moment to wash up. Then, please make your way to the dining room.

Josey Remembers Newtown

The gang filed out of Aunt Sunny's parlor to ready themselves for supper. As Josey walked, she thought back to the book General Hunt had given her about the Slaves of the Shenandoah Valley that had come from Ghana and the surrounding countries. In the book, there was a large group of former slaves who established a town called Newtown in the Harrisonburg area. And, by about 1892, Newtown was annexed to become its own proper town. Josey wanted to accept Aunt Sunny's offer of adoption. But, a secret thought welled up in her: *What if I have family in Newtown?*

Supper

The gang made their way to the dining table before Aunt Sunny arrived. Eric, entered the dining room, "The lady makes her apologies. Business has called her away for a short time, but she invites you to begin without her," he said.

The gang drifted into chatter. The younger girls, Lizzy and Rosie giggled and munched on the appetizer course of rolls and cheese, while the older ones reflected on all Aunt Sunny had said to them. "Can you believe all of this? Did you ever expect she would open her home to us?" Anne asked Billy.

"Honestly, I didn't. I knew she was a generous and kindhearted woman. But, as far as I expected, Aunt Sunny was a hardworking nurse working day and night to earn enough to eat and share the rest," Billy said. "Are you thinking you might stay?"

Anne sat up straight, "I just don't know," she said. "I've just lost Lady Kathryn, and I don't know about getting attached to someone. What about you? Anne said to Josey.

"Me?" Josey said. "Well, it *is* the prudent thing to do, isn't it?" Josey paused for a moment. "I see it's in my best interest to be formally adopted by Aunt Sunny, but the truth is, Newtown is calling me. What if some of my relatives are there?" Josey described some of the history she'd read. Josey wasn't the biggest talker of the gang, but when she did, she had the ability to draw everyone's undivided attention. "I'm certain my heart won't settle until I visit that place." Josey felt a tinge of guilt for her desire in the face of such a generous offer; nevertheless, she shared her heart honestly and trusted her friends to respect it.

"I'll go with you!" Anne said.

"You will?" Josey said.

"Wye, yes. It's perfect! I have business there—the trust letter from Lady Kathryn." Anne said. The girls discussed travel plans and determined to conceal their plans from Aunt Sunny.

The gang retired to staff quarters for the night. Josey took a glass of water to her sleeping quarters and placed it on the side table near her bed. She opened the drawer to find a small letterhead and fountain pen, just like the pen Pastor Jim used to use by the fire as he wrote his sermons. *I wonder how they're doing? I hope they aren't worried about me. I should tell them I am well. I should tell them about Newtown! Maybe they would want to visit?* Josey thought. She grasped the pen, dipped it into the fresh ink and began to write:

Dearest Pastor Jim and Lisa; ...

Ask Yourself

1. The Bible says God is good. What other simple truths hold true when life becomes scary or confusing?

2. Billy felt grateful and rejected at the same time finding out that Uncle John almost put him in the orphanage, too. Have you ever felt two feelings at the same time?

3. Considering that people who don't know God still have jobs and families, what do you think the Bible means when it says, "apart from Me [Jesus], you can do nothing." (John 15:5)

4. What do you think about Aunt Sunny's decision not to go retrieve the gang once she knew they were struggling to reach her? Is struggle ever a good thing?

Outdoor Survival Tips: Strange Encounters

Do you feel like you're being followed? When traveling alone—and even in groups—always remain aware of people in your vicinity. One good trick is to note a person's shoes (because people change their shoes less often than they change other attributes of their appearance). If someone seems to be in your area repeatedly without reasonable cause, do not attempt to confront the person. Neither should you proceed deeper into a nature walk. Instead, get to a safe populated location at quickly as you can—preferably one where safe adults are present, like a police station, school or restaurant.

Follow Billy's Journey

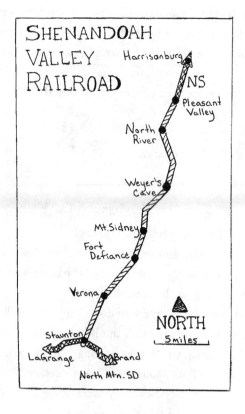

Chapter Eleven

Newtown, Virginia

A Baby Shall Lead Us

Dear Ma and Pa,

We made it! Aunt Sunny has an estate that goes on forever! It's so beautiful. She's invited us to stay with her forever. I wonder what Rosie and Lizzy are thinking?

Fredek has a new mentor, Don Wooden, Aunt Sunny's chief land developer. I think he's kind of worried about what Don might ask of him, but I think it will be good for Fredek to see what he's capable of. Heh, maybe I'm more like Aunt Sunny than I thought, because that's what she thought about us when she decided to let us journey to her instead of scooping us out of our difficult journey. Fredek is a great builder—just tree houses so far—but Don will teach him how to oversee large building projects all over the world.

Are there babies all around you in Heaven? What about all of the babies that pass away before they come forth from their mothers? Well, if there are, I'll hold them when I get there.

With love,

Billy

The Day Has Come

A few weeks was all it took for the gang to settle into new chore routines on Aunt Sunny's estate. Not surprisingly, none of them missed the old hand-to-mouth lifestyle. Even the pets made themselves at home. Rhea, the cat, had shifted her diet from field mice to fresh trout and scrap chicken; while, Rex and Virginia managed to create a new litter of eight *puppies!*

Josey postponed the trip to Newtown until her letter to Pastor Jim and Lisa had a chance to reach them. Finally, after three weeks of waiting, she told Anne it was time to go. Shortly after the girls agreed to depart the following morning, Eric approached Josey.

"Lady Josey," Eric said.

"Hello, Eric," Josey answered.

"A letter," Eric said, tipping his head and extending the letter.

"A *letter!?*" Josey said with excitement. "Oh, *thank you, Eric!*"

Anne peered over Josey's shoulder, as Josey read the letter. "It's from Pastor Jim and Lisa. They're coming to meet us in Newtown!" Josey told Anne. The girls felt even better about their plan and returned to their living quarters to pack.

The next morning, after the girls took off, Billy found Aunt Sunny to tell her about the girls' journey—just as they had agreed he would do. He found her in her parlor just after sunrise reading her Bible. "Can I talk to you for a moment?" he asked.

"Sure!" Aunt Sunny said, closing up her Bible to listen.

"Well, Anne and Josey took off this morning," Billy began.

"They did, did they?" Aunt Sunny said.

"They did, yes," Billy said. "They're headed for Newtown. Anne had some business to take care of concerning Lady Kathryn's trust, and Josey just had this inkling in her gut to see if maybe she might have some kin in that area. See, the people she used to work for planted a church in those parts going on about ten years ago, and she wants to visit."

Billy looked at the floor, not sure whether Aunt Sunny would be angry at his message.

Aunt Sunny thought before she spoke, which Billy was beginning to like. Then, she answered him in story, which he was also becoming partial to.

"I've lived a long life, Billy," Aunt Sunny said. "A few times, I witnessed as men and women saw visions on their death beds. One woman whose body was failing from tuberculosis spoke of seeing terrible demonic things. She'd had a miserably hard life, having lost her husband in a gruesome way during the war and suffered at his hand for many years before that. His loss left her with children ages four, nine and eleven to care for on her own, and it seemed the hardships had hardened her heart against man and God. I asked her, 'Do you want to walk with Jesus as your Lord?' She refused and died a few moments later."

Aunt Sunny continued, "Then, there was a wealthy lawyer with a similar experience. He saw ghostly apparitions and wanted nothing to do with the Jesus he had heard about. He told me he would return to this earth as a ghost to see to his many belongings. Believing this was impossible, I simply said, 'Well, Sir. Do not haunt *me!*' The gentleman died a few days after, separating from all his earthly belongings forever.

"See, Billy. I've lived here in Harrisonburg for a long time. I've tended men during war and assisted literally hundreds of births—most of them fatherless births of children whose fathers were torn away by war and hardship. I've seen young people—not much older than you—die in my arms, bleeding out and calling me Momma, because I was the closest thing to a Momma they'd ever known. So many opportunities I've had to bring orphans into my care, but I've never done so until now."

Billy loved Aunt Sunny's stories, but he was admittedly perplexed at how they related to the news he'd told her about Josey and Anne. She looked into his deep blue eyes knowingly and said, "Billy, these tragic stories have brought me to this point. She held his hand in hers. "I find myself now in a position to take in many children, and I wouldn't want to miss that opportunity again," Aunt Sunny said.

"I understand Josey's desire to have her questions answered, but since you all are in my care now, please tell me of any such schemes like this in the future," Aunt Sunny requested. "For now, I rest assured that Josey is in good hands with Anne. She'll need a strong friend with her for this journey."

"Wow, you really saw people die?" Billy asked.

"I did," Sunny answered. "We all did—us nurses."

"But why wouldn't someone want Jesus even right up at the end?" Billy said, innocently.

Sunny thought for a moment. "Many reject Jesus, and I'll never understand it. But many also have received Him and come to know that God's laws are good to give people abundant life on earth—even in the midst of their struggles. We don't always understand it, Billy. Then again, we don't need to," she said, smiling.

Billy felt amazingly light after unloading the secret he'd been keeping from Aunt Sunny. Normally, one for holding secrets close to his chest, he even surprised himself by wondering why they didn't just tell her in the first place.

The Past Meets the Future

Anne and Josey walked to downtown Harrisonburg where the letter had instructed them to meet Jim and Lisa for breakfast at the Horseshoe Restaurant. They wore their finest dresses and their heads high. The moment they entered, they saw Jim and Lisa standing just inside the door.

A rush of anxiety filled Josey. *I wonder if they're angry at me for running away*, she thought, but before she could do anything more, Lisa reached out and hugged Josey. Relieved, Josey remembered all of the freedom she had learned to feel along her journey. She spoke first: "How is the rest of the family—the children?"

"They're well, Josey," Pastor Jim answered. "We're happy to see you happy and well."

"Yes, we were so relieved to receive your letter," Lisa added. "Come. Let's sit and talk over a meal," she said.

At the table, Josey described her plan. "I'll be visiting Divine Unity Community Church—the church you planted—so I'm glad you're able to join. I've also reserved rooms for us at Hotel Rockingham just up the way, in case you'd like to secure rooms there as well. Anne here has a bit of business to address at Farmers & Merchants Bank on the first floor of the hotel building, and they're able to accommodate your horse and carriage if you'd like," Josey said.

"You've thought of everything, Josey. Thank you," Pastor Jim said.

"I imagine it will be quite special to step into your old church after being gone for so long," Josey said.

"That it will," said Pastor Jim. "But, believe it or not, that's not why we made the journey."

"It's not?" Josey said, surprised.

"Josey, we didn't expect to lose contact with you so suddenly," Pastor Jim began. Josey lowered her head in shame. "No no no," the pastor said. "We don't blame you at all! There's nothing to be ashamed of. Your journey to this place is remarkable. I just wanted to explain that the moment Lisa and I realized you were gone, we felt an intense regret that we had not told you everything we knew about your past."

Josey felt both comfort and shock at the pastor's words. "You know my family?" Josey asked.

"We do. And, as soon as we knew where you were, we knew we had to tell you," Pastor Jim said. "Your father worked for my father as an indentured slave for many years. As I grew, I remember him making music on any instrument he could find and leading his fellow workers in song. He was a seeker of truth and knew one day he would be free. He even talked to my father about his ideas, my father being a man of the faith considered his words heavily. I come from a long line of preachers, and by the time I was a young adult, my sister, Anastasia, had come to resent preachers for many things—chief among them, holding slaves. She fiercely rebelled against my parents, and she and your father began a secret relationship. She became pregnant and hid it as long as she could. When our father found out, he told his congregation and urged them to handle it well. But, the two young parents were shamed at every turn. After you were born, she and your father ran away to Newtown for fear the town might harm them. From what I hear, she abandoned your father not too long after that. Still reeling with pain and shame, she worked as a prostitute for some time before sort of just disappearing into the mist. I would be surprised if your father has any idea where she is to this day," the pastor said

"My mom is your sister? You are my—" Josey struggled to piece it all together. "Didn't your Dad ever go after her?" Josey asked.

"He tried to reach out to her," the pastor said. "I didn't realize it at the time, but he was on a journey himself, trying to reconcile his faith with society's standards. I remember conversations he and Anastasia had where she would argue that no one needs God to do good. Father would simply command her to stop speaking and end up so spitting mad that he wouldn't speak a word for days either. Those fights just pulled them further and further apart. He didn't know it, but we could see he was just daring her to leave," the pastor recalled. "Honestly, I think it broke her heart to know our father disapproved of her choice of men."

Josey chewed on these words in her heart for the rest of the day. She and Anne took off on their own and gave the pastor and his wife time to arrange their lodging. By sunset, Josey had still only begun to grasp all that she'd learned, but she was grateful to have gained more pieces of the puzzle.

Farmers & Merchants Bank

Bright and early the next morning, Anne and Josey set off to Farmers & Merchants Bank. The bank attendant who had setup their appointment greeted the young ladies at the door. "You'll be meeting this morning with Donovan James, our bank president," the attendant informed, showing the

girls to their seats.

"Thank you for meeting us on such short notice," Anne said.

"My pleasure," said Mr. James. "And, how may I be of service today?"

"My parents have established a will and trust at

this bank in my name, and I'd like you to provide information pertaining to the details of this most important document," Anne said, trying to sound sophisticated.

"Ms. Hudson," the bank president began, "my attendant did share this with me, so I have prepared a statement for you in advance." The president slid a paper across the desk to Anne. "You'll see that the total value is in the amount of $35,624, but keep in mind this amount does not include the stock gains from your 5 percent ownership in the Shenandoah Valley Railroad, which nearly doubles the amount in your bank account. This particular railroad hit a bit of a financial hiccup recently, or else it would be more," he added.

Anne, pretending to comprehend all she'd just heard responded to the one piece she did understand. "That is much more that the total I had anticipated, which was $31,624," she said.

"Astute observation!" the president replied, which thrilled Anne to no end. "Per your guardian's guidance, the monies were placed in a simple interest account, so the sum has increased at a steady clip," he said. "But that's not the whole of it. Remember, the railroad stock growth adds another $61,274."

Anne waited for him to explain if that meant what she thought it meant.

"That means your total net worth today is now $91,898! Young lady," he continued, "that's enough wealth to build several large homes—maybe even a town—and still own one hundred acres of river-bottom farmland!"

Anne, pleased and feeling confident replied in her typical manner, "Well, that should feed me, my cat Rhea, my dog Virginia … *and* her puppies!" With that, Anne and Josey stood and extended their hands to Mr. James for one final handshake. Just before exiting, Anne winked at Josey in a way that made Josey nervous for what orneriness Anne might have in mind. Anne turned to the bank president and said, "Sir, bein' as I am just a fragile little southern girl, might you tell me again what is a trustee?" Josey chuckled.

The banker answered, as if he didn't detect a hint of sarcasm, "But, of course," he said. "The trustee is the legal adult who has the right to spend your money to help you within the guidelines of the trust, which in this case was written by your deceased parents with the input of Lady Kathryn. Your trustee is responsible for distributing the funds to the stated beneficiary—in this case, … *you.* "

"And *who* is my trustee?" Anne asked.

"For that information," the president said, "you'll need to see the trust attorney at Sullivent Law Firm; or, if you're in a rush, your Aunt Sunny might know." Anne took down directions to the law firm Mr. James mentioned and headed that way.

Mr. Sullivent greeted the two at the door. "You must be Ms. Hudson," he said. My friend, Mr. James told me you would be visiting. Please, take a seat."

Anne inquired as to how much money she might be able to withdraw as a minor under the law. "Well, it looks here like the terms of your trust restricts you from taking more than 30 percent of the funds at this point, but you also have immediate access to your Great Grandmother's silver, an expansive thimble collection, a quilt and some sort of Greek mythology book for your own purposes. What else can I help you with today?" he said.

Anne was struck by the appearance of Mr. Sullivent. He looked exactly as she remembered her father looking. Forgetting her original question about the trustee on her account, she answered, "No, sir. Nothing further. Thank you." On her way out, Anne extended her hand for a closing handshake then, without explaining herself, hugged Mr. Sullivent like a long-lost brother.

Stunned, the man said, "Well, thank you indeed, young lady, and safe travels. Please come back if you have any questions at all in regards to the trust."

The girls had lunch in town then returned to Hotel Rockingham where they talked with Pastor Jim and Lisa about the next day's visit to Divine Unity Community Church.

Josey Finds Family

Unbeknownst to the group, Josey woke up before sunrise Sunday morning. She readied herself and left Hotel Rockingham quietly, being sure to disturb no one. *I just need a little time to myself to think,* she thought. She walked ahead, not knowing the town well at all, and found herself on Country Club Road in Newtown. *I think the church is near here,* she remembered. She gazed at a few of the houses leading to the church as she prayed for her stirring heart to find calm. Even with all the shutters pulled and all the townsfolk still asleep, she felt a sense of belonging in the community. *Everyone here has been so friendly and kind,* she thought. The morning was brisk with autumn air, and soon it would be full of the sounds of the many children in the town.

Josey's head hung low as she walked. It just felt right to lower her head to pray, and it also helped her watch her feet. When she heard a voice calling her name, her head jutted upward. At first, she said nothing. But, she heard it again, "Josey, come here. I need to talk with you."

Josey saw nothing but a lamb—one that looked so perfectly groomed she thought it must be someone's pet. Not a blemish to be found. Not a single speck of dirt. She thought, *I must need more sleep if I think someone's pet is summoning me,* so she headed back to the Hotel and into her bed with no one the wiser to her secret outing. She was pleased to find that Anne was still sleeping, and within minutes, Josey herself returned to dreamland.

Before Josey even realized she had dozed off, she awoke to the sound of Anne scurrying around the hotel room. "Time's a-wastin', Josey. Let's skedaddle!" Anne urged.

"Church isn't for another *four hours,* Anne!" Josey replied sleepily, sluggish from the hour she'd traded for exploration during the wee hours of the morning.

"We're meeting them for breakfast! Let's move!" Anne said, ignoring Josey's lack of enthusiasm.

"Fine," Josey conceded. The two collected themselves for church then enjoyed a fine morning meal with Pastor Jim and his wife.

"We still have a few hours before the service begins. Would anyone like to take a look around the town?" Lisa asked, not knowing Josey had already done some exploring herself earlier that morning.

"Yes!" Anne responded. The four walked up and down the town streets, enjoying the sounds of giggling children and the chirping of so many different bird species. Then, Josey heard another familiar sound—the summoning she'd heard that morning.

"Josey. *Josey!*" the voice called. Josey wondered if she were going mad and decided not to look for the source of the voice this time. Still, the voice rang out yet again.

"Do you hear that?" Anne said. Josey acted none the wiser. "Josey, someone's calling your name. What's back there?" Anne said as she walked toward the side gate of a nearby home and peered over the short fence. "Wye, there's nothing here but a little lamb," Anne reported back to the others. "Come and see!"

Lisa and the pastor walked with Josey to see what Anne had found. They commented on the lamb's thoroughly kempt coat. Just as Lisa leaned a bit in to pet the small animal, it spoke: "Follow me around back. There's someone you need to see."

Lisa yanked her hand back. "Did that lamb just ... *speak!?*"

Anne, remembering the strange behavior of the animals the gang witnessed on their journey, recalled how creatures spoke as they were closer to the vine. She explained this as best she could to the adults who had an understandably difficult time making sense of it all and eventually was able to convince them to listen. Unbeknownst to Anne, she had convinced Josey, too.

The group entered through the narrow gate and followed the little lamb to the back of the house where they found their old friend Gabe seated with a black woman about 70 years of age dressed in fine apparel no doubt for the Sunday service. On her side table sat a tin cup of steaming hot coffee and a brown leather Bible. To the right of those items stood a pot with a bright green vine—just like the vine on Reverend Timothy's land. Gabe's countenance was joyful, as usual. Gabe greeted the visitors then disappeared, leaving a few extra chairs in his place on which the visitors seated themselves—always the gentleman.

"Josey, I presume," said the old woman to Josey in a slow, peaceful voice.

"Yes, Ma'am," Josey responded.

"Well, I'll be. Aren't you a beautiful young woman," said the old woman.

"Thank you," Josey replied.

"—with those green eyes, like your father," the woman continued.

"You know my *Dad?*" Josey blurted out. The woman smiled and held out her hand, beckoning Josey toward her. The woman, although a stranger, beamed with a hospitality that gave everyone in her vicinity a sense of belonging. Josey took the woman's hand and stepped close to her side.

"Honey, I've known your father since he slept in my belly. He was quiet then, and he's quiet now. He don't always say what needs sayin', and that surely brought a share of grief his way. But, when your father met the Lord, the Lord read him like a book—just opened him up and read his soul. So, that man met himself when he met the Lord, and, I will say, if you see him worship, you'll know it. I'll say *that*," the woman said. "Now, Grace Josey, you know that means I am your grandmother—raisin' your father from a seedling of a man into the giant man he is today. I been prayin' to see you while I'm still on this earth. I can hardly believe you right here before me."

Josey didn't know how to react. She smiled at the old woman, who kept a grip on her hand the whole time. Josey had always imagined finding her father, but she had no idea she had a living grandmother—and certainly no idea that her grandmother would be praying to meet her. The moment lingered while Josey thought through all of this intensely behind the veil of her sweet smile, and the old woman gave her all the time she needed.

After some time, Josey said, "And you knew it was me?"

"I did. I did. Yes, I surely did," the woman said. "As soon as my gardener boy, Gabe, pointed you out from a distance, I knew. He said, 'Now, don't she look like the green-eyed girl you always prayin' about?' And, sure'nough, it was you. "

Josey looked to the garden behind where the woman had gestured and saw a boy bent over tending the soil. He looked up with a coy glance. *Gabe!* she thought—warmed by the realization that he was involved in her story. Josey felt how much this woman loved her, and her heart was inclined to receive it.

"So, I imagine you and your group is headed to Sunday service this morning?" the woman asked.

"We are," Josey answered. "These people," pointing to Pastor Jim and his wife, Lisa, "they used to lead that church. They've come all the way from Ladd to visit."

Josey's grandmother, knowing the girl's history, looked to Pastor Jim. The couple looked back knowingly. "A pleasure," the woman said.

"A pleasure," the pastor responded, tipping his head to the woman.

"Darlin', your Pa will be there this morning, and I expect he'll know you as soon as he sees your pretty face," the woman said. "And, you'll know him, too—the biggest man in town, with the biggest, deepest voice you'll hear like pipes in the air before you ever enter that church building."

Josey already had half expected to see her father at church, but to know it with certainty sent a rush of fear in with the excitement. Her heart was so tied in knots, that she wanted to run straight to church and run away at the same time.

"Well, you all get going now," the woman said. "I'll be seeing you, I expect," she said.

The little lamb that had led the group to the woman stood up from his cozy spot on the grass and walked between Josey and the woman to lead the group back through the gate.

"Do you think she knows that lamb can talk?" Pastor Jim said to the group, which had almost reached the gate.

"Well," Josey began, "if she don't, that lamb can tell her himself," she answered, smiling as the humor of it all set in.

Sunday Service

Anne, Josey and the Reverend and his wife approached the church building. Just like the woman had said, the sound of deep pipes spilled out through the white double doors propped open to allow the morning breeze to rush through the sanctuary. Inside, everyone greeted the new faces with warm handshakes. Anne had never been the minority at church before, but it didn't take long for her to forget that altogether. Those congregants from years ago who recognized the reverend and his wife embraced the couple and exchanged stories about their lives since last visiting.

The pastor took to the podium. "Welcome, all of you—old and new. Please rise and sing to the Lord the prayerful words of Miss Franny Crosby. The pastor motioned the congregation to open their song book and began to lead with large sweeping arm motions as the congregation sang Miss Franny Crosby's song based on Hebrews 11, "Whither, Pilgrim, Are You Going?"

Whither, pilgrims, are you going,
Going each with staff in hand?
We are going on a journey,
Going at our King's command.
Over hills and plains and valleys,
We are going to His palace,
We are going to His palace,
Going to the better land;
We are going to His palace,
Going to the better land.

Fear ye not the way so lonely—
You, a little, feeble band?
No, for friends unseen are near us:
Holy angels round us stand.
Christ, our Leader, walks beside us:
He will guard and He will guide us,
He will guard and He will guide us,
Guide us to the better land;
He will guard and He will guide us,
Guide us to the better land.

Tell me, pilgrims, what you hope for
In that far-off, better land.
Spotless robes and crowns of glory
From a Savior's loving hand.
We shall drink of life's clear river,
We shall dwell with God forever,
We shall dwell with God forever
In that bright and better land;
We shall dwell with God forever
In that bright and better land.

Pilgrims, may we travel with you
To that bright, that better land?
Come and welcome, come and welcome,
Welcome to our pilgrim band.
Come, O come, and do not leave us,
Christ is waiting to receive us,
Christ is waiting to receive us
In that bright, that better land;
Christ is waiting to receive us
In that bright, that better land.

The pastor motioned that the congregation be seated, then he opened his Bible. He said, "In the book of Deuteronomy, chapter 33 and verse 27, we read this:

The eternal God is thy refuge, and underneath are the everlasting arms: and he shall thrust out the enemy from before thee; and shall say, Destroy them.

"Let the people say Amen! with the assurance that the Lord holds you safe in His arms in the midst of trial. Let the people say Amen! with the assurance that the Lord giveth us all we need to endure in faith," the pastor said.

"Now, stand with me, as we proclaim the goodness of our Lord," he invited. The congregation jumped up and began to sing another inspired tune, penned by the same woman.

Safe in the arms of Jesus,
Safe on His gentle breast;
There by His love o'ershaded,
Sweetly my soul shall rest.
Hark! 'tis the voice of angels
Borne in a song to me,
Over the fields of glory,
Over the jasper sea.

Safe in the arms of Jesus,
Safe from corroding care,
Safe from the world's temptations;
Sin cannot harm me there.
Free from the blight of sorrow,
Free from my doubts and fears;
Only a few more trials,
Only a few more tears!

Jesus, my heart's dear Refuge,
Jesus has died for me;
Firm on the Rock of Ages
Ever my trust shall be.
Here let me wait with patience,
Wait till the night is o'er;
Wait till I see the morning
Break on the golden shore.

Josey heard a voice above all the others and was sure that it must be her father's. She saw the back of the head of a man who stood head and shoulders above his neighbors. *That must be him,* she thought. *Do I wait?* she wondered. She closed her eyes, hoping God might give her specific instructions on how to approach her father. The final verse ended, and she opened her eyes with no divine inspiration. The man was gone. *Oh, no!* Josey thought.

"Now, brothers and sisters, our brother has a song on his heart that I've asked him to sing for all of us." Josey looked on as the man she'd seen stood up from the seat just beside the pastor where to which he must have relocated while her eyes were closed. The man pulled his shoulders back and began to sing the African spiritual "Nobody Knows the Trouble I've Seen":

Nobody knows the trouble I've been through
Nobody knows my sorrow
Nobody knows the trouble I've seen
Glory hallelujah!

Sometimes I'm up, sometimes I'm down
Oh, yes, Lord
Sometimes I'm almost to the ground
Oh, yes, Lord

Although you see me going 'long so
Oh, yes, Lord
I have my trials here below
Oh, yes, Lord
If you get there before I do
Oh, yes, Lord
Tell all-a my friends I'm coming to Heaven!
Oh, yes, Lord

The man's strong voice filled up the sanctuary and poured out into the streets where the sounds of anguish plowed into the walls of the town buildings for all of Newtown to hear. Those who weren't in attendance looked up to see the source of the powerful notes. The musical outpouring so moved the town, it became known as the *Echoes of Newtown*.

The song concluded. The man, head down, glanced up directly into Josey's green eyes (which only her precise vision could detect) before he returned to his original seat for the remainder of the service. Her whole body froze when she saw the gripping green in the man's eyes, and Josey's gaze darted to the floor. She felted suddenly very exposed but was comforted when Anne reached over and grasped her hand.

After the pastor closed the service, the congregation migrated out slowly with lengthy greetings and joyful embraces among the townsfolk. The pastor and his wife shared stories with their old friends in the pews, while Josey and Anne pulled back into a quiet spot under the tree just outside the church doors.

"That was something," Anne said. Josey just looked at her with a slight nod of agreement.

The mountain of a man emerged from the boisterous crowd with slow thoughtful steps and approached the girls under the tree.

"Josey," he said.

Tears filled Josey's eyes and the breath rushed out of her. She hung her head and sobbed, realizing in an instant how unprepared she was for this moment—completely at the mercy of her broken heart. She didn't try to calm herself. She just melted into the tender little girl she had never been.

The man remained still while Josey cried. Silently, heavy tears fell one at a time from his caring eyes. Guilt weighed heavily on him with thoughts of how he could have protected his wife and daughter from the forces of the world determined to rip them apart—shame he'd laid down long ago at the cross but hadn't fully known until he'd known it in the presence of his hurting daughter.

"Josey, I'm so sorry for all this," he said in a soothing phrase. "I've missed it all—all your growin'. Ain't no words gonna make it right. I'm sorry you had to come find me, Josey. I should have come and found you."

Josey, picked up her gaze from the man's feet, to the top shirt button at his neck and finally made the swift jump to his eyes, which were waiting for her gaze to meet them.

"I should have come and found you," he repeated. He opened one arm, inviting her to his side. She just stared at him, her tears slapping the grass below like a summer shower. She thought about the grandmother she never knew existed, the loneliness she'd endured for more than ten years without parents, the knowledge that Pastor Jim and Lisa had kept from her the whole time, and she thought about the man in front of her—her Dad. Her actual Dad. At once, her heart caught up with her mind and she ran to him and reached around him as much as her little arms could reach around his tree-like torso.

"Better times-a comin', Josey girl," Josey's dad said. "They already here."

Anne made her way to Pastor Jim and Lisa to tell them the story she'd just witnessed of Josey and her Dads reunification. "It's amazing," Lisa said. "After all these years."

Josey and her Dad said goodbye with plans to connect again in the coming weeks, and Josey rejoined the group, who were trying to subdue their celebration about this monumental moment in Josey's life. They took turns hugging Josey who was still so moved by her interaction with her Dad. Then, Pastor Jim said, "So, we make our way to Harrisonburg, now, I suppose, correct?"

"That's the plan!" Anne answered.

"Well, let's head that way," the pastor directed. And, the group, led by Pastor Jim and Lisa took off toward the hotel. Anne and Josey followed behind, talking, when all at once Josey stopped and looked around intently.

"What is it?" said Anne.

"Do you hear that?" Josey said. "It's a *baby!*"

"I didn't hear anything," Anne responded without taking a moment to listen.

"Yes, it's a baby … right there in those bushes," Josey said, pointing to the bushes near the church. Sure enough, a dark-skinned baby, no more than one month of age lay there, wrapped in a loose linen blanket in the shade of the church bushes.

Anne called for one of the church women to come see to the baby. "We should take it!" Josey said.

"Josey, we're in no place to bring this baby on our journey. You've been through so much. Don't be a hero now. Let the women of the church tend to this little one." Like a swarm of happy bumble bees, the women scooped up the baby with a remarkable lack of shock and scurried back into the sanctuary where the baby was cuddled and cared for.

That night, Josey couldn't stop wondering about the baby. She prayed silently in her heart, *God, please be a father and mother to that little one with no one to care for it. Please see that the baby arrives to a safe place where it will find love forever.*

Back at the Estate

Breakfast at the estate was bustling with the members of the gang back together again along with two out-of-town guests and a few prominent business leaders. Aunt Sunny introduced everyone, "Children, these are the Moritz's and the Wooden's. And, all, I'd like to introduce our out-of-town guests, Pastor Jim and Lisa.

The table enjoyed an array of fresh eggs and meats from town and discussed their mutual heart and commitment to the plight of fatherless children. Anne found a quiet moment with Sunny while the table exchanged vibrant chatter, "Aunt Sunny?"

"Yes, Anne," she said.

"I wasn't able to discover the trustee of Lady Kathryn's will," Anne said. "The trustee holds the funds until I'm 18 years of age, but they wouldn't tell me who it is. Do you know?"

Sunny smiled. "Anne, your Aunt Tamara made me the trustee over the will and trust left to you."

Anne smiled back. "I hoped it was you," she said.

"You amaze me, Anne," Sunny said. "You certainly do amaze me."

The table continued discussing tactics for meeting the needs of children left orphaned after the war. The adults were pleased to see such passion from the gang to meet the needs of such children and talked about the best ways to help their visions come to pass.

Mr. Wooden knew from experience how to craft orphan rescue villages in a way that incorporates agriculture, animal husbandry and the hopeful message of Christ, and this captivated the gang with excitement—especially Fredek who was naturally gifted in building—but the other adults spoke over one another. The focus of the fellowship seemed to shift from fatherless children to accomplished adults.

"Whoa," whispered Billy to Rascal. "It's getting a little tense in here for me."

"Yeah," Rascal said. "Are these men or mosquitos? They're biting like ... well, like *us!*"

Aunt Sunny overheard the boys and smirked at them. "Let's all remember the cause at hand, gentle people," she interjected with firm grace.

Just then, Gabe entered the dining room with a wicker basket, which he delivered directly to Aunt Sunny with a quiet comment no one could hear. "Thank you, Gabe," she said. Sunny reached into the basket and pulled out a tiny infant—the same child Josey had seen by the church. The presence of the baby brought all of the bickering to a sudden halt. The stress of human ideas seemed to evaporate into the heavens and was replaced with a calm assurance in the wisdom and creativity of God. Sunny snugged the swaddling garments of the infant and raised it slightly into view of the guests. Josey felt in her heart that her prayer had been answered and smiled knowing the baby would be at home in Aunt Sunny's loving care. Sunny gazed at the infant and said, "A baby shall lead us."

Ask Yourself

1. Josey and Anne took off to Newtown without telling Aunt Sunny. What did Billy mean when he thought he felt lighter after telling Aunt Sunny of the girls' plan?

2. Aunt Sunny saw tragedies when she was caring for people during the war. How do you think her sense of *purpose* affected her choice to keep going?

3. Anne isn't allowed to take out her inheritance funds until she's 18. If you were Aunt Sunny, would you make Anne save the money, or give the fortune to Anne when she is 12?

4. Josey learned so much about her past from her trip to Newtown. How do you feel learning that no one shared with Josey the story of her birth family?

5. Anne has always been compassionate with Josey, so were you surprised that Anne told Josey not to be a hero with the infant Josey found in the bushes? Why do you think she said that?

Survival Tips: Business Meetings

The meeting over breakfast at Aunt Sunny's started out well and got a little hairy when the group started listening to their own voice above that of others. That happens without entering meetings with the proper mindset, but leaders who exhibit good character in meetings get the best out of themselves and others.

Here are tips for leading an effective meeting.

- Prepare a list of the things your meeting will accomplish. This is called the "agenda."
- Too many people can actually harm the progress of your meeting. Check the attendee list and make sure only those who are really necessary are invited.
- People first. Respect others for what they can teach you—regardless of their position (above or below you in rank). And, respect everyone's time by honoring start/stop times.
- Keep conversation on topic. If it's not on the agenda, say, "Let's address this matter further after the meeting." Then, set a time to follow up.

- Surprises are for birthdays, not meetings. So, if you have any big revelations, consider giving attendees a heads-up by including it on the agenda or sending out a note separately.
- Assign someone to take notes that include action steps and the person who has agreed to take those actions. Then, make sure you quickly do everything you agreed to do in the meeting and report back. This will set a great example for the rest of the team to do the same!

Follow Billy's Journey

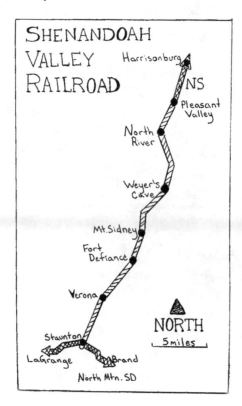

Chapter Twelve

From Far and Wide

The Grand Celebration

Dear Ma and Pa,

When we started this journey, a ball was just one of those things that blacks your eye if you don't swing at it. Turns out, it means something altogether different to the fancy class. It's a party, and, don't tell the girls, but I can't hardly wait.

Aunt Sunny's throwing a ball for all of us. She's inviting her friends from far and wide. There's a fella here in charge of teaching us all how to dance. Dance!

Aunt Sunny has everything set—from our fingernails to our breeches (new ones for the ball). She said, when we were children we were taught to be seen and not heard, but at this ball, she wants us to address her friends directly. She's teaching us how to behave nice and proper-like, "listen to understand" and "extend your hand in greeting," so I'm repeating those until they sink in. Wish me luck with all of the shiny folks afoot.

Don't worry about Rex. He's loving life. He took a walk with me under the stars a few nights ago. I wondered for a moment what I'll do when he dies, but I didn't want to think about it. For the first time, though, a new thought swooped in. I have Rascal now—a real brother. I have more family now than I can count.

In Psalms 36:6 My Sunday school teacher taught us in the Bible that God's righteousness is like the highest mountains, His justice like the great deep You, Lord, preserve both people and animals. I looked up the Hebrew word for "preserve" in this verse and it means to save from moral troubles. Any dogs up there? Just curious because I know my dog Rex will someday join you and Mom.

Love, Billy

The Announcement

Breakfast became a welcomed rhythm for the gang who enjoyed knowing each morning would start with a full belly and familiar faces. One morning, as the gang was gathered around the morning table, Aunt Sunny stood up. Fredek, the last to notice, took a swift elbow to the ribs from Billy to let him know everyone was waiting on him to attend to the lady of the house.

Sunny addressed the group, "Children, your presence is a cause for celebration. As I mentioned on your arrival, you'll be attending a Victorian Ball—not only attending, but hosting—to commemorate this new family."

Rascal, who always liked baseball, shot Billy an ornery glance. "Not *that* kind of ball, kid," Billy said.

"This is Charles, whom you met on your first arrival. He is an accomplished master dancer and the man who will teach you … I'm sorry, Charles. *What will you teach them?* Sunny asked.

Charles smiled, "Thank you, Miss Sunny. The dances we shall learn are four: The Waltz, the Virginia Reel, The Grand March and the Soldier's Joy." The girls bounced in their chairs as they heard the news. "Of course, I have trained with the world's finest for many decades, but I have high hopes for what we can accomplish in ten days."

"*TEN DAYS?*" Billy exclaimed.

"Billy!" Sunny reacted, startled by Billy's volume.

"Oh, sorry, Aunt Sunny!" Billy said quickly. "Is it true that this *ball* takes place in only ten days?"

"Indeed, it is! The out-of-town invitations have been sent and likely received by now, and I have plans to extend the invitation to the whole of Harrisonburg" Sunny answered. "You're right, Billy. We will have a house bursting with guests in fewer than two weeks." She paused and looked around at each face at the table. "Shall we get to work?" she said, smiling.

"First, you, Anne" Sunny said. Anne's eyebrows lifted. "You will be our event coordinator—from decorations in the main hall to seating, lighting and music. You will keep the bird's eye view and delegate tasks to our able-bodied gentlemen here as necessary," Sunny said, gesturing to Rascal, Billy and Fredek.

"Really?" said Anne. "Are you sure you want me to do all of that?"

"More than sure, Anne," Sunny said confidently. "You are fully capable. And, I've asked my footman, Eric, to assist you in anything you might need."

"Now, Rosie dear. I would love it if you would compose fliers that we may post throughout Harrisonburg. Write them in your best script and decorate them with your creative sensibilities," Sunny said.

Rosie was surprised to be given a role at her young age; although, she was passionate about illustration and writing. Deep down she had always wished someone would ask her to do something like this. *Yes!* Rosie thought to herself. "May I get to work right now?" Rosie asked.

Sunny laughed but regained her composure. "Of course, you may, Rosie. You'll find supplies in my office."

Rosie bolted from the table then walked quickly back to push in her chair the way Sunny had taught her. Rosie stood upright, said, "Excuse me please," then slid both hands down the front of her apron as she had seen the adults do. She proceeded to walk most maturely to Sunny's office, but once out of sight, her speeding footsteps echoed back to the breakfast table.

I've always wanted to write something important! she thought as she hurried to the office.

"Fredek," Sunny said. "Don Wooden is ready to begin work with you after breakfast to prepare the grounds for our guests."

"Me?" Fredek said, listening for the first time. "That's great!" Fredek joined Don, the land developer, around 9am. The two discussed plans to relocate large bushes to accommodate the most carriages near the home.

"We'll also find a new home for this cotton gin," Don said to Fredek. Cotton gins came into popularity about 40 years earlier, "your Aunt Sunny has no need of one," he said. Over the next week, the two-man team dug a thousand shovels worth of dirt, moving almost one hundred bushes and crafting a welcoming entrance. "Fredek, I've scheduled you a day off, son. We have a few hours of work today, leveling out that hole over there. But, tomorrow, is yours."

"I appreciate it, Sir," Fredek said.

"So, take up that shovel, and follow me," Mr. Wooden instructed. Fredek picked up a shovel in one hand, a bucket of water in the other and followed Mr. Wooden to a large crevasse in the earth left by years of water erosion from rainfall at the entrance of the house. "We're going to fill this deep crack. Don't want any guests falling to the center of the earth," he said.

"That doesn't sound too hard," Fredek said.

"It's not. Not at all … once we get the dirt," Mr. Wooden said.

"Whu—Where's the dirt?" Fredek asked. Mr. Wooden pointed to a plot of land at the back side of the house about 20 yards away. "Oh," Fredek said. He looked at a perfectly fine piece of land that would be less of a hazardous location for a hole. "At least when the job's done, we're *done!*"

"That's right," Mr. Wooden answered, receiving the water bucket from Fredek and taking a long swig of the water warmed by the sun. The two dug until an hour past noon until they had unearthed nearly enough dirt to fill the hole. Down in the fresh hole, Fredek raised his shovel for one last pile of dirt, but when he struck the earth, frigid water gushed forth.

"DON!" Fredek yelled, as he struggled to exit the deep hole. "HELP!"

Mr. Wooden quickly dropped flat on his stomach at the edge of the hole and reached out his arms. Without saying a word, Don gripped Fredek's outstretched hand and pulled the boy's massive frame from the pit.

The water rose so quickly that Fredek was soaked to the knees. He took a seat against the home for a moment to collect himself. "That came out of *nowhere,*" Fredek said.

Don, looked down at the boy, then to the pit they'd made, which already had filled a few feet with water. "That's one problem solved, one to go."

Fredek suddenly realized what a terrible situation he was in. "Oh, no! The water! How do we stop the water? If it keeps gushing like this, it will flood the whole house! What have I done!"

"Now, take a minute, son. Do you think the Lord is stumped on this one?" Mr. Wooden said calmly.

"You mean *pray about it?*" Fredek said. "Does God care about some ol' flood?"

Mr. Wooden smiled and reflected back, "Do God's *children* care about some ol' flood?" Fredek just looked at him. "Fredek, maybe you've been told religion is just a bundle of rules, but that's not the heart of it. God knows you and wants you to know Him. But, you can't get to know someone without talking." Fredek nodded. "In the meantime, let's see what we can do down there before this land turns to river."

Fredek rose to his feet, and as he did so he shared his heart with God as best as he knew how. He whispered a bit and thought a bit more. *Listen, if this isn't interesting to you, God, just let me know,* Fredek thought. Then, like lightning, an idea struck him.

"Do we have a pipe? A *big* one?" Fredek said.

"We do at the back of the house," Mr. Wooden said. Fredek ran to fetch the pipe. He returned and jammed it as hard has he could down into the center of the pit, with the force of a jouster from Medieval Times.

"Well, what're you doing there, son?" Mr. Wooden said. "That was a perfectly fine pipe.

Fredek felt his superhuman strength pulse through his arm as he released the pipe. It plunged forth through the rising waters and down several feet through the source of the fount until it hit a bed of clay below the surface. At once, the water stopped rising from the ground and now channeled only up through the pipe.

"Oh, I see what you did, boy. Here, let's thread this cap onto the end of the pipe," Mr. Wooden said.

Fredek hadn't known that Mr. Wooden had an end cap on hand but was encouraged that the perfect solution presented itself. "PERFECT!" Fredek yelled over the roar of the water shooting 15 feet in the air and landing back into the small pond that had formed. Fredek's super strength enabled him to attach the cap against the force of the water, and the roar of the waters suddenly turned to silence.

Fredek and Mr. Wooden, both drenched and covered in mud, stood for a moment without speaking—just watching the pipe, half-expecting the cap to shoot off a mile high. After a few minutes, reality set in that the solution worked. They both breathed a big sigh of relief that spilled into uncontrollable laughter.

"You know, Mr. Wooden, I did what you said," Fredek confessed. "I told God how nervous I was that I would ruin the whole event—the whole *house* for that matter. I kinda think maybe He heard me. More than that, I think maybe He *cared*. And, somehow that doesn't seem quite as crazy as I thought it would."

"Ha, son. Wye, that sounds like the beginning of a good relationship to me," Mr. Wooden said. "I'd like to say our work here is finished, but remember that crevasse we needed to fill?"

"I almost forgot," Fredek said.

"Yep, it's *still* there. What'ya say we finish what we started?" Fredek found the tools, which he'd flung all different ways during the chaos. He loaded his shovel and began the long work of leveling the ground at the front of the house.

The next day, Fredek, returned to admire the work with Mr. Wooden. As they looked on Mr. Wooden looked at Fredek and said, I reflected last night on why God gave you and I favor. Hmm, said Fredek. Please explain. Well, you, me, and God teamed up to solve the problem. The Bible says a threefold cord is not easily broken. Son, never forget as you amass wealth and influence throughout your life to bring others along with you to get help along the way.

Billy Reflects

A few hundred yards away from the previous day's water fiasco, Billy found himself in between jobs and chose to enjoy his window of freedom under the crown of the sycamore trees where a little pond shined nearby. Rex, who had been running free all morning, made his way to Billy's hand for a good pat on the belly. "Don't that remind you of Mr. Pickett's pond, Rex?" Billy said. "That's where we used to do our thinking, isn't it, boy."

Billy stared out onto the water and continued his conversation with his trusty fur-friend. "I guess we're both domesticated now, huh boy. It was fun though, wasn't it?" As much as Billy took pride in his success in bringing the gang to the end of the road, he felt a little sadness thinking that his adventures were finished. Billy rubbed Rex's head like he was starting a fire, which Rex always loved. "I know, boy. You didn't much like that wolf. I didn't either. That wolf scared the wits out of me, in fact."

Billy thought to himself, *it is good not to be scared anymore. Even though we could probably handle a whole pack of wolves this time ... if we ever got the chance.*

"Don't get me wrong, Rex. I'm glad we made it here, I am! But ... well ..." Billy wasn't sure how to put words to his fear that the gang might never adventure together again.

Rex broke Billy's thoughts with his loud bark alerting Billy that a carriage approached from a few miles up the road.

"HOLY, MOSES, REX!" Billy shouted. "It's TIME!"

The Guests Arrive

Back at the house, the girls put the final touches on the home then hid in their dressing rooms to ready themselves into their formal gowns—each designed specifically for its wearer. No one was to see the gowns until the official presentation of the gowns.

Major Corbin and his wife (Later he would be elevated to Brigadier General of the U.S. Army) directed the fulltime staff at the estate who were tasked with maintaining a safe event. Each man reporting to the Major was brimming with impeccable character, love and humility.

Fredek, Billy and Rascal were charged with valeting the carriages and greeting the guests. "I see a bunch of fancy people, but no one I recognize just yet," Billy said. "I'll take this one," Billy said, gesturing toward an upcoming carriage.

Just then, the land filled with carriages descending from the sky, translocated from all different parts of the country. "What's happening!" Billy said, a few paces away from the others.

Rascal caught a glimpse of Gabe out of the corner of his eye. "I think I know," Rascal said.

Gabe appeared in the midst of the boys. "How do you do, fellas?"

'GABE!" Billy said, startled. "You did this." Gabe only smiled.

"But how did that piano get in there? Gabe asked. The boys bent their heads to peer into the great hall. Sure enough, the cryptic piano from the inn at Pleasant Valley was displayed in the corner. Stumped, they looked back at Gabe. "Shall we welcome the guests?" Gabe said with a smirk.

Guests included Mr. Wooden who brought his lovely wife, Melinda—both dressed in diplomatic garb from their latest stint at the orphanages they'd set up for Miss Sunny in Africa; trust lawyers from Newtown, the Sullivents; oil barons from Ladd, Mr. and Mrs. Willis; Billy's school headmaster, Mr. Shapleigh and his elegant wife; his band director, as well, Mr. Brandt (along with every student in the town band); Joshua, a friend of Billy's from school in Ladd; Joey the clerk at Pleasant Valley Inn; Dr. and Mrs. Phillips from Ladd; Sisters Maria, Louada and Claire from the monastery; Reverend Timothy and Mama Carol from the North River; and Pastor Jim and Lisa, back from Berryhill. Hundreds more guests from all walks of life, dressed in their finest, filled the great halls of the estate to celebrate the children's adoption.

"This is nearly everyone we've ever known," Rascal said.

"Did you see Sister Maria?" Fredek said. "She's wearing shiny pink dancing shoes."

As each new attendee entered, the boys announced the guests, just as they'd been trained to do. Soon, the hall was filled with more than one thousand exquisite guests who shared Aunt Sunny's joy in welcoming the once-orphaned children into a permanent family—not only hers but the one family of God.

The student-led orchestra took its place, instruments in every hand, and began to play. Woodwind, brass, percussion and even stringed instruments joined in harmonious melody, as Mr. Brandt raised his baton to lead the famous Civil War march, "The Battle Cry of Freedom."

Presentation of the Gowns

The orchestra crescendoed into a grand finale, which led into a single trumped tone that called all guests to attention. The trumpet blew out a succession of beats, drawing guests attention to the grand staircase for the presentation of the gowns.

Sunny ascended the stairs to address the crowd. "Greetings and gratitude to each of you for joining this celebration. Now, as we present the young ladies of the family, please pay close attention. Each gown is a unique creation by our beloved seamstress, Mama Bush, crafted specifically for the special girl wearing it, down to the color.

Rosie walked to the center of the staircase. She wore a beautiful yellow gown. "Presenting, Rosie!" Sunny said. "Rosie's gown is sun yellow, representing the angel Jophiel who is said to oversee the thoughts and wisdom emanating from the throne room of God. Rosie stepped to the edge of the staircase.

Josey took her place at the center of the staircase. "Presenting, Josey!" Sunny said. "Josey's exquisite gown is cobalt blue, representing the angel Michael, the leader of all angels. Josey, stepped to the side to join Rosie at the edge of the top stair. In the crowd, one man stood above the rest. "My *Dad* is over there!" Josey whispered to Rosie.

Anne stepped slowly to the center of the staircase in her flowing red gown. "Presenting, Anne!" Sunny announced. "Red, here, represents the angel Uriel who is said to oversee healing for God's people. Thank you, Anne," Sunny said.

Little Lizzy skipped into view, causing the crowd to giggle in one cohesive rumble, which suddenly reminded Lizzy of the vast sea of people at the bottom of the stairs. For a moment, she froze. "This way!" Anne called. Lizzy snapped out of her momentary stupor and smiled as she walked toward Anne. "To the middle!" Anne said.

Lizzy took her place at the middle of the staircase. Her gown was angelic and white. "And, presenting our precious Lizzy," Sunny said. "Her dress represents the angel Gabriel, who we know for overseeing the revelation of God on earth."

As the girls descended the long staircase in unison, the audience erupted in boisterous applause, praising and thanking God for bringing these children into the fold of God, nesting them into family on earth and keeping them safe on their journey of faith. The girls took comfort in knowing they had a guardian angel with them through every adventure. They also took comfort in having selected male mentors with the counsel of Sunny over the weeks leading to the ball. These four men (General Hunt, Old Man Milton, Josey's dad and Reverend Timothy) awaited the girls at the bottom of the staircase. To their surprise, the gentlemen offered to lead each young woman in her first dance. Josey savored every moment of the waltz with her Dad, while Anne realized that General Hunt's peg leg didn't slow him down one bit on the dance floor. Every minute of the girls' dance training paid off in spades for the young ladies who moved like clouds across the floor. The crowd was captivated with the meaning of the moment.

Following the dance, Sunny addressed the crowd: "Please greet the girls as you are able and continue to enjoy the orchestra. The evening's gourmet offerings include donated delicacies of lemon-gingerbread, cider cake, rhubarb rolls and orange custard from Bazzle's. Please also enjoy morsels of carved roast, apricot-glazed turkey, also donated by our town butcher, circulating throughout the room," Sunny invited.

"I'd like to thank the Methodist Church of the Shenandoah Valley region who prepared fresh vegetables and donated more than 50 pounds of Dutch-style country cheese," Sunny added.

"Finally, be sure to taste the flip," Sunny said.

"Flip?" Fredek questioned.

"Yes. *Flip!*" Anne said, "Lady Kathryn sipped it occasionally. It is a fancy tea—akin to an egg cream with rum and ale."

"At this time, I open the floor for tributes." Sunny scanned the crowd for anyone who might be moving toward the stairs to join her midway up the staircase to speak a tribute. She saw a young man moving from the area where the orchestra was seated. He made his way to her. "And, what's your name, dear?"

"I'm Joshua, Ma'am. I know Billy Vogt from school in Ladd," he answered.

"Wonderful!" Sunny exclaimed. "All, this is Joshua, a friend of Billy's." The crowd quieted down and listened intently as Joshua spoke.

"Billy," Joshua began. He hesitated for several seconds, shocked at the attention of so many faces. With trepidation, he continued, "Billy, we, all of us back in Ladd, ... uh, we want you to know your life is an example for us." He gained confidence as he spoke. "An example of perseverance and bravery to us all. From your story, we realize that we can do anything with your God—that your God can be our God, in fact," Joshua added. "I mean, you know as well as any that we ain't the fastest, the tallest, the keenest minds ... but God's eye is on us like it's on all of you." Billy nodded, largely stunned by Joshua's touching words. "We just wanted to say 'thank you' for showing us what it looks like to trust in something real."

"Thank you, Joshua," Sunny said, though no one heard her words over the roar of the crowd. "Thank you," she said again, as the crowd began to settle. "Many have called these young one's rebels, but it's true: they are children of exceptional conviction and courage. And, you, Billy are a young man with distinct leadership ability. As Sunny spoke, the inspired piano, which Gabe had made sure to include, began playing "It Is Well With My Soul." Moved by the moment, Sunny prayed:

Heavenly Father, thank you for William Henry Vogt, the leader of this unlikely gang. We are humbled to receive him into the family as our gift and blessed to call him family. We dedicate this son of promise wholly to You with an expectancy that you would grant him the Spirit of wisdom and revelation, so he might know you better, like Paul prayed in Ephesians chapter 1 and verse 17.

We pray he is a man who does not walk in the counsel of the wicked or stand in the way of sinners nor sit in the seat of mockers, and his delight shall be in Your will as young David hopes in the first Psalm.

Grant him clean hands and a pure heart that he would not lift up his soul to any idol or swear by what is false, just as David asks in the twenty-fourth Psalm. Let him live in freedom to be a voluntary servant of God, just as Peter writes to the exiles in his first letter chapter 2 and verse 16.

Lord, if it be Your will that he finds a wife, we pray they would complement each other as they fulfill Your purposes on the earth. Above all, for Billy and all of these children, we pray that they may know you, the one true God, Jesus Christ whom You have sent, as Paul attested to Colossians, chapter 1 and verse 10. And, may he know Your Spirit who brooded over the surface of the waters before the world was with form, as we read in Genesis the first chapter and verse 2.

Sunny finished her prayer which came to be known as "A Son's Blessing" and said, "Now it's time to fight for the fatherless with love and not the sword." (She didn't realize she had reiterated General Hunt's words from weeks before.) "This estate has more than 1,000 acres of undeveloped land, Billy young man of promise, use it to spread the Gospel of Jesus the Christ."

"Assemble your workers and build a wall around this land, marking it as a safe haven and central post from which your gang will minister to kings and beggars alike."

Billy hadn't been expecting such a prominent spotlight. He made his way to the staircase where Joshua and Sunny still stood. Sunny quietly asked him to say a word or two to the crowd—whatever he wanted to say. He turned to face the throng: "Friends, gentlemen … ladies. Apart from Christ we can do nothing. I read in an old journal my Grandfather often said, "Christ is All." I knew that in my head when we began this journey, but now, I know it in my heart, as well. That is something worth celebrating."

In the meantime, Mama Carol had made her way to the staircase. "I just want to say one thing, Miss Sunny, if that's alright with you."

"Of course!" Sunny answered.

Mama Carol addressed the crowd, "As head of the debutante committee in the North River region, I would like to formally invite Miss Anne, Miss Josey, Miss Rosie and Miss Lizzy to join as the newest members of the Shenandoah Valley Junior Debutante Society." The girls, who were still standing near their mentors were stunned and giddy to receive such an invitation. "Our members are taught how to be wonderful ladies of society both culturally and spiritually, as they serve their communities. Won't you join us?"

The girls all shook their heads yes. "They've accepted!" Mama Carol shouted from the staircase in a most ladylike fashion. The girls walked quickly back to the staircase to thank Mama Carol as she descended. Anne was the first to hug Mama Carol. "Won't you please play us a tune?" Mama Carol asked.

This moment for Anne was the culmination of all of her lessons from Lady Kathryn. Anne's heart filled with nervousness, but she tamped it down and nodded affirmatively to Mama Carol. Anne stepped to the piano. She played "Fur Elise"—the most treasured work of her late aunt. It rang out like chimes from heaven—every note perfect rhythm and intensity. At the conclusion, she stood and took a bow, then another. She looked at Lizzy, knowing Lizzy was supposed to have a song prepared to sing.

"Now is the time," Anne whispered to young Lizzy.

"I can't. I can't do it," Lizzy mouthed back to Anne—afraid to say the words she had prepared to sing disappeared. It was like something had struck her with amnesia.

"You can," Anne said. Then, she ascended the staircase once more and announced in a loud voice, "Please welcome our dear sister, Lizzy, to sing."

With no choice but to sing, Lizzy joined Anne on the staircase where Anne whispered a few encouraging words before rejoining the crowd below. Lizzy, unsure her voice would obey her wishes, opened her mouth and readied her breath. "Here goes," Lizzy thought to herself. Her eyes closed as she sang:

> *O beautiful for pilgrims' feet,*
> *Whose stem impassioned stress*
> *A thoroughfare for freedom beat*
> *Across the wilderness!*
> *America! America!*
> *God shed his grace on thee*
>
> *Till paths he wrought*
> *Through wilds of thought*
> *By pilgrim foot and knee!*

Startled by cheers of the people below her, Lizzy looked up. She took a small bow and stepped down into the mass of guests. Rosie, her diminutive friend in life, rushed to her side and asked, "Where did you get that song?"

"I … I don't know," said Lizzy, puzzled. Lizzy scanned the room with her eyes and caught Gabe looking right at her. His smile solved the mystery. Lizzy had received a gift from heaven.

Not one for large crowds, Rosie stood at the house entrance where she witnessed all the events of the evening—from Sunny's words, to Joshua's tribute, Anne's piano piece and Lizzy's vocal performance. Sister Maria, who had been several paces to Rosie's side, had noticed. She approached the girl. "Rosie, I have something for you," said Sister Maria.

"Oh, Sister Maria, I didn't know you'd come!" Rosie said. Just then, Rosie remembered how suddenly she departed the monastery without even so much as a goodbye, and she felt a bit of guilt. "Oh, Sister. I didn't say—I'm sorry I—"

"My child. Don't worry yourself," consoled Sister Maria. "There is no harm done. Though, I have a letter I was saving for you. Surprised by your departure, I haven't been able to give it to you until today." She handed the letter to Rosie.

Rosie looked up at Sister Maria with eyes that begged confirmation, "for me?"

"It's yours, child," Sister Maria said.

Rosie read the letter:

Our darling Kristen Rose,

My heart will break daily remembering this day on which I placed you at the monastery. I am 14 years of age and seeking the best hope for you. I thank God for you, though I am unequipped to raise you up.

May you trust in the Lord with your whole heart, leaning not on your own understanding, and in all your ways acknowledge Him that He would make your paths straight. You are a gift.

Mother

Rosie couldn't believe it. "You met her?" Rosie asked.

Sister Maria shook her head. "No, child. She was already departed." Rosie hung her head. "The blanket in which she had wrapped you had this." Sister Maria handed Rosie a worn piece of cloth, embroidered with the phrase *I love you to Lawrence and back.* "The best the sisters and I could estimate is Kansas. She may have ties to Kansas."

Rosie smiled and nestled in close to Sister Maria. A bit overwhelmed by the letter and flickering with feelings of love, hope and abandonment, she just needed a hug—nothing more.

A Familiar Face

Back inside, Old Man Milton had worked up the courage to ask Miss Sunny to dance. He stepped toward her and reached out his arm just as another man stepped between the lady and Mr. Milton. "Shall we dance, my lady?" the other man said.

Sunny, who, distracted by guests, had been unaware of both men, turned suddenly to the man requesting a dance of her. "John!" she said.

Without wasting a beat, John, Sunny's estranged husband from Ladd, swept her up into the rhythm of the orchestra. Sunny, opposed to his return in her mind, brushed against the comforting familiarity of the moment, dancing with her husband. She knew nothing could come of it, being as he was slave to his substances, but she gave herself a song's worth of time to decline him.

As they danced, John whispered, "Oh, Saundra. I've been terrible to you. I took alcohol as my companion instead of you. I haven't had a drink in months—not one drop—and I never will whether you'll have me or not. But I sure hope you will."

Sunny listened in disbelief. *Could it be true?* she wondered. She spoke to him as they danced, finally agreeing to inquire with the townsfolk as to the changes they have witnessed. "I have a house-full now. I can't just go taking on a man with a vice, you see."

"And, I wouldn't ask you to," John answered.

Sunny was struck by her inclination to trust him. She resisted her urge to answer quickly and abided by her better judgment to check his story against those who have seen his transformation firsthand.

"If this is true, John, what you say," Sunny said, "well, it'd be a miracle!" John just smiled as they danced the next song.

"I believe in those," he said.

The Next Mission

As the orchestra continued to play Billy noticed a sealed letter had made its way to his pocket. *That's odd,* thought Billy. He looked up and saw Gabe smile at him and he knew it was from the Heavenly Father. He opened the letter immediately, it was short but the directive was clear. "Anne, let's assemble the team we have a new mission." Billy said in a confident voice.

"Oh, and Anne, trust me this next mission is a longer journey but will be much easier in an Alkebulan sort a way." "Right, Billy" said Anne, rolling her eyes as each member of the gang had already assembled behind her in a show of support.

In the Next Realm

In the deep recesses of the evening, the music echoed into the woods. Gabe stood at one of the highest points in Virginia, Reddish Knob, just five miles south of Sunny's estate. He watched over the property, as he tended to do. From the beginning, his job was clear: look after the fatherless wanderers of the world. So far separated from all people, Gabe extended his wings. They extended many yards to each side with a soft glow around the edges that revealed creatures lurking in the distance. The orange-eyed creature, the same one that had been carried off during the gang's journey, stood watching the ball from a lower vantage point than Gabe's.

Gabe started to take off in flight to sweep the creature up and away before the children ever knew they were in danger, but he stopped, looked up then simply remained at his post, watching over the joyful festivities.

"Someone called you off?" the orange-eyed creature communicated to Gabe.

Gabe felt no need to respond concerning his orders. Instead he said, "Your master brings isolation, but God's children find family in Him."

The Secret

So, what was the secret to Billy's past. Well, I'll tell you myself. Discovering God's love for me was akin to meeting my own Mom and Dad from a different time and place. I always wondered if my Pa would send me back if he could save

his wife instead. And, that wonderin' didn't make me feel much wanted. The secret to it all was a surprise to me.

It isn't my Ma or my Pa's choice that decides whether I'm worthwhile, God decided that long ago. He picked me, like he picked everyone else on this earth.

God put each person together in the right body in the right time of history. There are no mistakes when it comes to children. There just ain't. And, I, for one, thank God for that.

Ask Yourself

1. What did Fredek learn about prayer when he encountered the water fiasco the day before the ball?
2. Why do you think the girls worked with Sunny to choose a trustworthy male mentor? Do you have a role model in your life you can trust?
3. Joshua took inspiration from Billy's courage to seek answers to his deepest questions and learned that all have the ability to do the same. What questions do you wish you had answers to?
4. Aunt Sunny's prayer talked about idols. What are idols?
5. Aunt Sunny wouldn't agree to remarry Uncle John until she investigated what his neighbors had seen of him over the last few months. How will talking to the townsfolk help her know if John is trustworthy and being honest with her?
6. Billy always wondered if he was chosen. What did he find out?

Survival Tips: First Dance

Lots of organizations hold dances (schools, small towns, community clubs), so here are a few things to consider when you're getting ready to attend one.

- Tell an adult what time the dance starts and ends and of any other plans before and after, including who you expect to be joining you.
- Alert an adult if any part of the plan changes.

- Resource a book, video, counselor or friend who can teach you a few basic steps that will fit the type of dance you're attending.

- When in doubt, be kind. It's normal to feel awkward at social events. Believe it or not, that's why manners exist—to give people a plan of action when their feelings don't match the environment. For example, say you enter an auditorium full of students dressed up. You see people grouped together, but you're unsure whether you'll be accepted. Try approaching someone else who is by him- or herself and simply greeting them with a "Hi." If you're feeling extra brave, compliment the person's attire: "Nice shoes." Odds are, the person will thank you and maybe even start a conversation. But, even if that person is rude back, you can be proud of yourself for making the room a kinder place.

About the Author

Blake Fite has spent most of his career working to defend the cause of the fatherless in both the U.S. and abroad. He recently finalized a writing project about secret truths learned from those without parents. His next book in the *Carriage Kids Book Series* is already in the works.

Blake Fite currently lives and works with his wife Laura and two children, Samuel and Rachel in Tulsa, OK.

Two Ways to Support
Hearts of the Father Outreach

It's easy to stand with the ministry of Hearts of the Father in memory of the Moritz's three little ones and in faith for the many children in need of family around the world.

1. Sponsor a child. Click here to be a sponsor of one of their orphanages: http://heartsofthefather.org/donate/
2. Go to www.globafamilyresources.com/shop and purchase some extra copies of the book to give away to kids who have lost a parent. The book is designed to help kids process loss and a percentage of the net proceeds goes directly to Hearts of the Father Outreach.

CARRIAGE KIDS WRITERS CLUB©
HEALTH AND INNOVATION FOR THE NEXT GENERATION:
A Program of Global Family Resources

FOLKS, THERE IS A PROBLEM:
Broken families affect all areas of society—from healthcare, to education, to employment, to poverty. But, even more devastatingly, that

brokenness can plague a person's life for generations. Here are just some of the ramifications of family breakdown in the United States:

- More than 400,000 children currently live in the U.S. foster care system—without the security and support of a family.
- The American Psychological Association (APA) reports that between 40 and 50 percent of first marriages in the U.S. end in divorce.
- When divorced couples marry again, the divorce rate increases (APA).

BROKENNESS IS THE STATUS QUO:

But, GLOBAL FAMILY RESOURCES SAYS WE CAN DO BETTER!

The Carriage Kids Writers Club© equips young adults to thrive!

WHAT IS THE CARRIAGE KIDS WRITERS CLUB©?

In 2018, Blake Fite assembled a group of young students to exercise their creative skills as first-time authors, and the result was the 2019 book: *Echoes of Newtown* (the first in the *Carriage Kids Series* of books). The book chronicles the wild journey of a runaway orphan gang in search of *true* family—and processing their loss along the way. So much more than just a good read, *Echoes of Newtown* challenges searchers of truth with therapeutic discussion questions to consider alone or in the presence of a safe adult. Plus, each chapter has real-life survival tips!

Originally, the goal was to get this book into the hands of every foster-care resident in the state of Oklahoma, but the vision has grown!

GROWING THE NEXT GENERATION OF WRITERS

OUR TEAM THOUGHT... If this original group of students collaborated to produce a book of adventure and healing, why not do more than just distribute the book? Why not teach other young people how to write their own book?!

HOW CAN I GET INVOLVED?

Join or sponsor a young adult today! Members receive monthly content to launch the writing journey!

They'll also learn ways to channel their thoughts and emotion into the written word for the benefit of themselves and others! Additional benefits include the opportunity to submit writings for print and compete with others on the authorship journey.

PLUS ...

Healthy youth become healthy adults! Become a member of the CARRIAGE KIDS WRITERS CLUB© and HELP BREAK THE CYCLE OF BROKENNESS!

YES! Please sign me up to be a part of the Carriage Kids Writer's Club! Just go to the following website and register today:

www.globalfamilyresources.com/kidsclub

Special Thanks to Our Sponsors

Our sponsors made this book a reality. The one thing that binds each one of them together is in one way or another they have helped the cause of the fatherless. For that I am grateful for their contributions.

- www.heartsofthefather.org
- www.morganjamespublishing.com
- www.sflegalgroup.com
- www.valleywaymedia.com
- www.changealife.net
- www.donordepot.com
- www.crossroadsoftulsa.com
- www.globalfamilyresources.com

CPSIA information can be obtained
at www.ICGtesting.com
Printed in the USA
JSHW021919261120
9810JS00006B/8